ESSAYS FOR AROUSAL
VOL. I

ESSAYS FOR AROUSAL VOL. 1

A Collection of Historical Romance Novellas

J.R. WALKER

J.R. Walker Publishing, LLC

Contents

To my dearest daughters, may you one day discover a love that tran-
scends time and echoes through the ages.

I

Elizabeth's Story

It's 1807.

The elderly Lord Darby, Earl of Lincolnshire, has recently married a wealthy young heiress. Having no sons from his first marriage, he is desperate for a male heir.

His young wife is entirely devoted to him and his cause. Yet, a chance encounter with a member of her husband's staff changes everything.

The 8th Earl of Lincolnshire was considered one of the luckiest men in the south of England. It wasn't often that a man just shy of seventy-two years married a beautiful, young heiress. Indeed, most men that age were already in their graves, but Lord Darby had one desire in mind that kept him young: he needed a son. Having been married to his first wife for thirty-five years with only three daughters, he yearned to pass his title to his own male blood, not through the marriage of one of his daughters. And who better to give him a son to assume the title than the now Lady Elizabeth Darby, the only child of one of Britain's wealthiest silk merchants.

The young Elizabeth had married the elderly earl when she was but eighteen years old. She, of course, resisted the marriage, seeing as her intended was older than her own grandfather would have been at the time had he been alive. But she did take hope in knowing that she would be a young widow with a title—something her family had never had within their grasp until now.

But after three years of marriage and still no son, the earl started getting disheartened. The wedded couple performed their conjugal duties every other day following luncheon, except on Sundays and when Elizabeth's courses were due. During that week, Elizabeth relished in her freedom from the shackles of being the earl's bedmate.

It was not that Lord Darby was cruel or even aloof to her. Indeed, they had established a friendship in their three years of marriage—albeit a formal one. The problem was that the earl only performed his marital duty for his benefit and his alone. Elizabeth would almost give in to sleep every time they coupled were it not for his pained grunts and frequent drinks of brandy to keep him going. Given what her maid had told her as she dressed Elizabeth for her wedding night, she had hoped for more. But alas, the maid had been misleading, and Elizabeth regretted she had even asked what to do in the first place.

Of course, Elizabeth knew that this was her burden as a wife and had never given much thought to it being any different until the day she stumbled upon the stable master for the estate. Her courses had come that morning, so she was free to go riding after lunch. She rarely rode, as it seemed to please the earl more if she were somewhere nearby. But she yearned for fresh air and some distraction outside the walls of the house.

The stable master would never have expected her, as it was widely known that the earl and the countess retired most days following lunch for several hours. But, out of character, she had decided to go riding. When she got to the stables, however, he was nowhere to be seen.

Recalling that he held a small living space on the backside

of the stable, she walked around the stables and up to what she assumed was his front door. As she lifted her hand to knock, a noise halted her fist in mid-air. She held her breath, waiting to hear it again. She detected a soft giggle, then a low purr, followed by the unmistakable sound of wooden posts creaking along an old floor. Forcing herself to breathe so she did not faint from suspense on his doorstep, Elizabeth forced herself to move softly to another side of the stone dwelling. Not knowing why she was pursuing the sound instead of turning away as a lady should, she crept to the open window that looked through a modest living space straight to a bed.

There, the stable master, known for his long, curly brown hair and bronzed skin from the sun, was doubled over a fair, buxom woman whom Elizabeth did not know. Standing with his feet firmly on the ground, he pushed himself into the woman slowly and deliberately. One of his hands was above her head on the bed while the other held one of her soft, pale legs. Elizabeth knew she should avert her eyes, but she was entranced by the entire scene: the muscles in his buttocks contracting with each thrust, his strong hand on the woman's soft thigh, but most notably, the way she seemed to absolutely enjoy what he was doing to her.

Finding the resolve to step away quietly before being caught (although she thought to herself that she was not the one who should be ashamed), Elizabeth walked swiftly back to the house, trying to rid her mind of what she saw—and what she felt. Her maid had told her that she would feel a readiness between her thighs when it came time to consummate her marriage to the earl. But the feeling never came to her. Until now.

Locked in her bedroom with the door shut and her head leaning against it while she caught her breath, she felt a deep and intense throbbing between her legs. What was more, she felt wetter than she normally would on this day of her courses. She wanted to move her hips so the feeling would intensify, but instead, she tried to will the image from her head and force the yearning out of her body.

...

By November of that third year of marriage, Lord Darby was growing weaker and was frequently forced to bed due to a racking cough. But after a week of respite following the most recent illness, the earl joined her for lunch as usual, his energy restored.

"We shall resume our conquest this afternoon," he said with spirit as they left the dining room to lounge in the drawing room.

"I am afraid we cannot, my lord. The timing will not allow for it."

Knowing exactly what she meant, Lord Darby stopped walking and dropped his head. With a heavy sigh, he said, "I suppose it is not meant to be then."

"Don't give in so easily, John," Elizabeth said tenderly, resting her hand on his forearm. She only used his given name when they were alone together. "You were so unwell all last month. It is no wonder your seed did not take. You have your energy back now, so I am sure with more rest this week, we will have better luck soon."

But he shook his head again and looked sadly into her eyes. "I am afraid it isn't in the cards for me, my sweet. I don't blame you, of course. It seems that I will never have a son of my own. Sometimes when I have these bouts of illness, I think I am done for anyway."

Elizabeth felt genuinely sorry for him. And in truth, she was also sad for herself because she did want children at some point. Indeed, a child would be a very welcome diversion from the loneliness that engulfed the hollow house she now called home.

Seeing that the earl was settled in his room for an afternoon rest, Elizabeth set out to ride. Or at least, that is what she told her husband. He had smiled at her, commenting on how when he was feeling better, he would love to see how her riding had improved with her frequent outings. Had he been a healthier man, Elizabeth would have worried that he might indeed recover and uncover that she hadn't been on a horse once in the last few months but instead was focusing her studies elsewhere.

Since first stumbling upon the stable master and the woman

in a compromising scene, Elizabeth had watched them at least six more times. She figured out that they met every Thursday when the woman delivered fresh washing to the stable boys and the estate's gamekeepers. The woman was the daughter of one of the earl's tenants who worked alongside other women in the village as laundresses. Elizabeth assumed she was only slightly older than herself, given that she was unwed and still under her father's roof.

Each time she watched them, she felt increasingly disgusted with herself. She could not figure out why she went and would hate herself for it the entire long walk back to the house. She would block the scenes from her mind and force herself to do something with her hands, like embroider or pen a letter to her mother. But then, as the next Thursday would get closer, she would get hungry to observe...and to feel.

Heading to the stables for what would be her seventh Thursday in a row, Elizabeth took her usual route back behind the stables to the stable master's lodgings. But when she slyly approached the window, the bed was empty. Feeling her breath quicken, she looked around in the window to see if they had migrated to another area of the dwelling. After all, she once found them wrapped around one another in the doorway between his bedroom and what she assumed was the rest of the lodging.

Seeing that the bedroom was empty, she quickly started backing away, and as she turned to head back to the stables, she bumped into none other than the occupant himself. She fell directly onto her back, her feet going right out from under her. It was like hitting a wall.

"Countess!" the stable master said. "My deepest apologies. Are you all right?"

Elizabeth could hardly make out his face in the bright sunlight that had morphed into a halo of gold around his hair. Taking the arm extended to her, she said, "My goodness, you caught me off guard. Yes, yes, I am fine."

But she wasn't fine. She was teetering between feeling completely embarrassed for being caught spying on him in his home and irritated that she found herself here once again in the first place. Dusting herself off, she put on a smart smile and tried to recover her dignity.

"I was looking for you, actually."

"I would hope so, seeing as you were looking in my house, my lady," he said somewhat coyly.

"Right," she said, trying to buy herself a moment.

"Is there anything I can do for you?" he said, pressing her.

"Yes," she said matter of factly. "I am in need of riding lessons, and I have it on good faith from my husband that you are an impressive rider."

"I certainly hope that is the reputation I have, given it is my occupation, Lady Darby."

"Right," she said again, feeling completely knocked off her feet, which, of course, she just was. "Would today be a fine time to start?"

He shifted his stance and said, "Seeing as you are my employer, I, of course, need to be available to meet your request."

"But you obviously have other duties to attend to?" she said, pressing him, knowing full well she may have placed him in an uncomfortable position with his usual Thursday companion.

"On the contrary, I was going to go out for a ride on one of the newest members of our stable yard, Jasper. He is young and has had poor training up until now. But he is of excellent stock, so naturally, I have every faith he will do well here."

"I will ride him then," she said, feeling a burst of confidence in her riding ability.

"With all due respect, ma'am, Jasper needs to be thoroughly vetted before I allow you to ride him."

"Nonsense," she said dismissively. "You underestimate my riding abilities."

"Well, seeing as you are here for riding lessons, I assume you are admitting that you need to hone your horsemanship skills," he retorted.

Elizabeth paused, trying to see how to not let him best her.

But saving her from her own tongue, he said, "Might I suggest you ride your horse?"

"My horse?" she asked, dumbfounded.

"You have a horse here in the stables. A wedding gift, or so I was told when she arrived three years ago. She's beautiful. And rarely ridden, obviously. She will do well to have someone become familiar with her. Here, follow me," he said, turning back toward the entrance to the stables.

Elizabeth followed carefully, noting how muddy the path was and how she evidently was unaware of it when she was pursuing her initial errand.

Finally catching up to him, they walked into the stables and strolled along the different pens. As he halted, she looked over the fence to see a brilliant white muzzle looking down at her. Mesmerized, she reached up to stroke the mare's face. She looked deeply into the brown eyes, then removed her glove and brushed her soft nose with the back of her hand. The mare sniffed her gently and then stepped as close as she could get to Elizabeth through the fence and turned her face to see her better. The two locked eyes. All the while, Elizabeth never stopped stroking her.

"You are breathtaking," she whispered to the horse. She laid her cheek next to the mare's. Elizabeth inhaled deeply, allowing the familiar scent of a horse to conjure images from her childhood of riding her horse, Penny. She felt herself instantly love this creature.

Drawing back, Elizabeth looked to open the gate. The stable master intercepted her, pulling the door ajar so she could walk in. Elizabeth never took her hand from the horse as she looked her over. The mare had a perfectly white coat, aside from a speckling of grey spots on her back and haunches. She was pristinely groomed, and her muscles were strong and capable. As if living in a dream, Elizabeth grabbed reigns hanging from the wall next to her and gently slipped them over her muzzle.

"Let's see how we do together," she whispered, then she grabbed an empty water pail, turned it over, and stepped up on it, throwing her leg over the mare. Once settled on the horse's back, she grabbed the reins and squeezed the horse on either side, clicking her tongue to encourage the horse to move. In a wave of fluidity, the mare started forward and nuzzled the stable master as she emerged from her stall.

"Right," the stable master said, clearly at a loss for words. "I shall just follow you then."

"No need," Elizabeth said, still entranced. "We will just be getting to know each other today. We shan't go far." And with that, Elizabeth allowed the horse to take her out into the pasture.

After several laps around the pasture, Elizabeth felt her legs growing fatigued with the effort of staying centered on the horse without a saddle. Knowing that if she went much longer, she wouldn't be able to dismount on her own, so she steered the mare back to the stable yard with little effort. It was not lost on her that it was as though this horse could read her mind, much like Penny once did.

The stable master, having watched her from the stable yard the whole time, met her and took the reins, tying the horse up to the fence for grooming. He then brought out a proper stool so that she could get down. Elizabeth shakily slid down from the mare's back. But instead of landing firmly on the top step, she felt her feet slip to the bottom step, and her legs nearly buckled, except that he caught her with one arm. She laughed unreservedly as he steadied her on her feet.

"Are you all right?" he asked hastily.

Still laughing, she replied, "I'm certainly all right. I'm perfect, in fact. Thank you for catching me." Holding onto his arm a moment longer, she looked him in the eye and continued, "Regrettably, I am no longer as fit as I once was when I would ride every day. Married life has softened me, I'm afraid." Then, letting go of his arm, she walked somewhat shakily to a bucket to grab a brush to start grooming her.

"Ma'am, allow me. That's not necessary."

"Oh, it absolutely is," she said dismissively. "This is just another way she and I can get to know one another."

Not knowing what to do with his own hands, the stable master grabbed another brush and began stroking her mane. The two worked in silence for some time, and then, breaking the silence, he said, "You clearly are not in need of riding lessons."

"One can always learn new tips and techniques." But after a pause, she conceded, "No, I do not need formal instruction per se. I spent my childhood on a horse's back." The two kept working, moving toward the horse's haunches.

"Her name was Penny. She was my closest friend."

Knowing full well how wonderful it was to find friendship in animals, he replied, "I am sure she was the steadiest of friends."

"Oh yes, she was. Always waiting for me, never passing judgment. Listened to anything I needed to say. And was the most worthy escape from the world outside of us."

Coming to the same side of the horse, he said with sincerity, "I am sorry you had to escape your world."

She looked at him intently and nodded her gratitude. Turning away from him, she could still feel his eyes looking at her. "What is it that you want to say?" she asked.

Checking himself quickly, he took a step toward the front of the horse and said, still looking at her, "You're just...unexpected, ma'am."

"How so?" she asked as casually as possible, but she realized that she wanted him to be surprised by her.

"Well, for starters, you have incredible horsemanship skills, and yet you have never once ridden or visited the stables until recently. I have also never seen a horse take to another person the way she did when you met. She instantly trusted you, which says a lot about your character."

"Did you have concerns about my character?" Elizabeth asked, feeling somewhat defensive but trying to stay nonchalant.

"Well, ma'am, you are the countess, and we never saw you. So naturally, the staff have formed opinions of you, which, of course, are unfounded."

"What opinions?" she pressed him.

He shifted uncomfortably and said, "That's not for me to say, as I never had thought about you. My job is strictly with the horses. People aren't really my specialty."

"Oh, is that so?" she blurted out before she could stop herself. He looked at her, surprised.

"What I mean to say is, you are employed by my husband and me. Therefore, you are a people person first, are you not?"

"I suppose so," he said, somewhat confused. Elizabeth knew she was once again trying to cover up her past misdeeds of spying on him with that woman, so she quickly changed the subject.

"What is her name?"

"Who?"

"This horse, of course. Who else would I be asking about?"

He continued to look at her, the brush in his hand stilled as he searched her face.

"Majesty," he said hesitantly.

"A fitting name for her, I should think," she said. "I assume she earned that name because of her majestic appearance and persona and not because the staff believed her owner was rumored to have a distasteful disposition?"

He smiled broadly and said, "You really are not what I expected." Then, he added, "I did not have the pleasure of naming her, but I believe she does indeed claim that title in her own right."

She handed him the brush, gave Majesty a final stroke, and then said, "I will ride her every afternoon, and I would like to start riding in the woods and will need you as a guide. Will your schedule allow for that?"

"It will be the most important event of my day, ma'am."

"Please call me Elizabeth. If we are to spend our afternoons together, I would much rather be her than this 'ma'am' or 'Majesty' I have become as the earl's wife."

He hesitated and then nodded in agreement. She started to pull herself away but then said, "And what shall I call you?"

"Gregory, ma'am."

"Gregory," she said softly. "Thank you for today."

As she turned to take the long walk back to the house, she felt her smile radiate across her face as she reminisced about the feeling of being back on a horse—and a special one at that. And, as she went to bed that night, she couldn't help but think of Gregory and found herself whispering his name to see how it felt rolling across her lips.

...

As fall began to give way to winter, Elizabeth stayed true to her commitment to riding Majesty daily with Gregory. The two rode hard most days, but sometimes they took leisurely rides through the forest, following a creek bed still high with water from heavy autumn rains. During their rides where they meandered for hours, Gregory told Elizabeth about how he had come to work for the earl, and both shared memories about growing up on horseback. He told her how he worked in another stable with a small landowner, learning under his father. As a young boy, Gregory would make dolls for his sisters out of horsehair that he would pull from the brushes after grooming. He said he knew even in the moment that they were nothing close to what his sisters might like to own, but he felt so proud to give them all he had.

When coaxed, Elizabeth even opened up about her childhood, sharing how her father had been unpredictable and her mother had always bustled from one event to the next. She shared how Penny had been her source of stability and comfort and how she had so yearned for that stability once Penny died. Especially since she had gotten married.

As much as Elizabeth loved Majesty, she couldn't help but ignore a growing fondness for Gregory as well. He was so gentle and kind, mannerly even. And yet, she also knew another side of him that left her feeling unsettled and confused. Every day that he would gently lift her down from her horse at the end of a ride she couldn't help but think of how his muscles would swell with each thrust into that woman. And she couldn't understand how his character, which on the outside seemed so proper, could allow him to behave in such a way with a woman who was not his wife. Of course, she knew that the marital act was not just for marriage, and she was certainly not naive enough to assume that no one ever did it outside of marriage. But she couldn't get over her surprise that they were clearly doing it because they *both* wanted it.

Thoughts of this woman who had captivated Gregory consumed her more and more. And with each ride they took, she found herself swallowing the question burning her tongue. *What is she to you?*

But that question was answered, to her shock, one Thursday when Elizabeth showed up late for riding. The earl had been in good spirits that day and felt well enough to sit in the library with her after lunch. She tried not to constantly check the hour, knowing that she needed to be there to listen to his stories, but she didn't want to be rude to Gregory either. Finally, she told the earl that she just wanted to send a message with her maid that she would not be attending her riding lessons as usual. Lord Darby told her she shouldn't miss out on his account. He commented on how well her complexion was now that she was riding more but cautioned her not to get too much wind exposure as it might rouge her cheeks. Elizabeth accepted the compliment gracefully and thanked him for his company. Then, trying not to run out of the library with excitement, she slowly walked out of the house after pulling on her riding habit and then all but ran to the stables. In her haste, she missed the ominous rain clouds that were building behind her.

Flushed and breathing heavily, she walked into the stables, ready to apologize for her tardiness. However, she was caught completely off-guard by two women talking to Gregory and the two stable boys under his management. The boys were smiling broadly, clearly enjoying themselves in the company of these two slightly older women while Gregory offered each of them ale. He looked up as he heard the commotion of her footsteps and instantly walked around the group, gently touching one of them on the elbow as he moved in her direction. It was *her* elbow.

In a moment, Elizabeth sized up this woman who had obviously captured Gregory's heart. She had thick dark brown hair spilling under her white cap, and her skin was shockingly pale in contrast to her hair. She was soft and buxom, and she could tell she had a big personality based on how she was laughing with the stable boys and how the other woman had little to say. Elizabeth thought this woman was opposite herself in just about every way.

As Gregory approached her, she felt a coolness take over her face and body, and she stiffened as he drew near.

"Where is Majesty?" she asked.

"She is in the pasture. When you did not show, I figured something had waylaid you, and you wouldn't ride her today. I put her there so she could take her exercise."

"Well, I am here now, so I would like her readied for my ride."

"I will need a few moments to saddle her and Jasper."

"That is not necessary. I will ride alone."

"But...," he started to say but then seemed to think better of it, clearly assuming that her displeasure was that he did not have her horse ready. Let him believe that was the case, Elizabeth thought. "Would you like ale while you wait?" he offered somewhat sheepishly.

"Thank you, no," she said swiftly and turned to walk to the pasture to wait for him to ready her horse.

Majesty was saddled in no time, and as Elizabeth started to mount her, Gregory said, "Are you sure you do not want company?"

"I am perfectly capable of riding on my own," she snapped.

"Rain is coming. You won't want to be long."

"Then I best be fast," she said. Before she could give it a second thought, she swung her leg over Majesty's back and straddled it between her thighs. She would ride like a man today. She kicked Majesty's flanks, snapped the reins, and the pair took off through the pasture gates as the first raindrops fell.

Elizabeth couldn't ride fast enough away from the scene. How dare he display that kind of behavior? And in front of her? He knew she was there when he touched that woman's elbow. To show that kind of...familiarity. She was aghast. And hurt. But she couldn't ever show him that. She didn't have a right to be broken. She knew that. He wasn't hers, and she was married! And he was just an employee in her husband's house—her house.

What hurt her the most was that he clearly didn't have any thoughts of her. It broke her because she spent every night thinking about him as she fell asleep. In her head, she had created a fantasy life that she was the woman he desired and loved, and she had almost started believing it the closer they got on their rides. She felt sick with disgust for how she could be so occupied with a man other than her husband.

Consumed by her rage, she didn't realize the rain was now starting to come down in sheets. Slowing Majesty, she looked around, trying to gauge her surroundings. She had ridden this path so many times, yet it all looked the same with the rain. She had no real idea how far she had ridden and knew she needed to find shelter. But she also knew she couldn't turn back. Not just yet. She wasn't ready to explain herself. Not that she had to, but Gregory would want an answer for her briskness.

Starting to shiver, Elizabeth turned Majesty around on the path and started her with a trot so she didn't slip in the mud.

The rain was coming down even harder now, and Elizabeth felt the water dripping down her back. Her hands were growing numb with her icy grip around the reins. Debating whether or not to find shelter under dense shrubbery, she began to make out a figure racing towards her. *Gregory.*

"Are you mad?" he yelled, throwing his hood from his head as he came upon her. She chose not to answer him with words but found the strength to sit taller in her saddle and looked at him piercingly. "A woman of your obvious intelligence should know better than to press on in rain like this!"

"I was on my way home, as you can see!" she shouted back at him through the pounding rain.

He rode up next to her, turned his horse, and began to offer her his cloak, which was significantly drier than her own.

She refused to take it, shouting back, "Nonsense, I am fine!"

He looked utterly aghast. "Have I done something to offend you?" he asked, throwing his cloak over her shoulders despite her refusal.

She looked piercingly at him, and then, to both of their surprises, she burst out laughing.

"Why ever would you think that?" she said through her laughter.

"I may be just a meager servant in your house, ma'am, but I am not dumb. And I like to think I can read people well," he said. And then, as though an afterthought, he added more quietly, "I believe I have come to read you quite well, too, Elizabeth."

Her face fell with a seriousness that matched his words. "Oh yes, it would appear you know people quite well."

His expression told her that he had caught onto her meaning. And his silence told her he had no idea how to address her now. Accepting his silence as proof of his affection for that woman, she squeezed Majesty's flanks with her legs and started to ride again.

The pair rode through the sheets of rain that continued to fall between the trees over their heads. Elizabeth refused to show signs of weakness or an inability to finish her ride and maintained a steady pace. With the stable in sight, she slowed Majesty so she did not slip in the mud that was thick in the yard. Finally entering the cover of the stable, she threw the reigns over Majesty's neck, and they were instantly caught by Gregory. He had quickly dismounted and was there to help her down. But while he was tying up her horse, she swung her leg to dismount, but her legs did not catch her, and she crumpled to the hay-covered floor.

In an instant, Gregory picked her up in his arms and began to carry her behind the stables. She had little fight in her, as her limbs were so cold and stiff, and she was doing everything in her might to keep her jaw from chattering. He was taking her to his cottage.

Gregory's house was the simplest dwelling she had ever been in. There was a large wooden table with two chairs, a stone fireplace with a single chair facing it, and a bed. He placed her in the chair in front of the empty fireplace and began to pull her boots off. With some effort, both finally came off, and he then reached up her skirts to pull down her stockings. She immediately stiffened and found her voice, saying,

"How dare you?" But her voice had little of the strength she hoped, and her chattering teeth certainly didn't help her cause. He looked at her with exasperation.

"You can barely move your arms with how chilled you are. I wouldn't dream of offending you in any way, including the ultimate offense of letting you freeze to death. Unwrap your arms so I can pull off your cloak," Gregory commanded.

Elizabeth did as she was told, and in moments, she was undressed down to her shift. He quickly placed the blanket that had covered his bed over her shoulders and started a fire. Within a few moments, the flames began to blaze. After ensuring the fire was sound, he took off his wet clothes down to his breeches and undershirt and laid out her clothes in front of the fire. He then sat on the floor next to Elizabeth and put his hands up to the heat.

Silence hung between them for several minutes until he finally said, "Her name is Alice. She is a laundress in the village. She brings the laundry on Thursdays for all the staff that serve your household."

"We have several laundresses in our employment, none of whom are from the village," she said quickly.

"Indeed, laundresses that work for you, doing your washing. But someone has to do our washing, as we haven't the means or the time, and yet we have to look well-kept."

Elizabeth bit her tongue. Why had she never taken the time to learn the interworkings of her own house? She supposed that she felt like it was never really hers to know about. It was always her husband's and his first wife's home. She felt like an intruder into the home they had once held together, so much so that she refused to sleep in the former lady of the house's bed chamber and opted for what would have been a prominent guest's room.

"It didn't appear that she just brought your laundry around."

He paused, and then, reading into her eyes and no doubt seeing that she knew more than she was letting on, he said, "We both fill a need for the other. Or did, rather."

She looked at him as he said this, waiting for him to expand, but it never came. "What changed?" she asked finally.

"I lost what free time I had, and our timing never aligned anymore to be, well, to see one another."

"You mean you lost your free time to me," she said bitterly.

"My time with you has become the most important part of my day," he said firmly.

"Yes, because I am your employer. Naturally."

"No," he said. "Riding with you has surpassed any other...obligations or diversions."

"Nonsense, I am fully aware that I supplanted your time with that woman and that it in no way compares to what you used to do with her."

He looked intensely at her.

"First of all, she is not *that* woman. She is Alice, and she is a good woman. She may not be of high birth, and she may be willing to spend time with me, but that does not make her a woman to speak of distastefully."

"There can be no discussion of taste when it comes to a woman who can be so...free of her principles," Elizabeth said firmly.

"Elizabeth, she is a widowed woman who lives with her elderly father. Her young husband passed away two years ago. What transpires or transpired between us is not as immoral as you are making it out to be."

"Why not marry her if she is a widow?"

"I can't afford her," he said simply. "And she doesn't need a husband for economy anyway. She runs a successful business on her own now."

Elizabeth envied the woman even more, thinking of the freedom she apparently carried. But then she thought about her own position and how one day she too would be a widow and would likely have no need for another husband either.

"You gave reasons for why she did not need you, but if you had the means, would you marry her?"

He thought carefully but then said with what Elizabeth felt was genuine honesty, "She would make a fine wife, but I don't need a wife. Perhaps I have held out for something more but never believed it was there."

"Believed?"

"Yes, believed. Love is just as fantastical for someone of my rank as yours, I imagine."

"But that is to suggest your opinion has shifted on the matter?"

He paused for some time, choosing his words. "I have seen what it means to care for someone more deeply."

Elizabeth couldn't find the words for what she wanted to say or know next. And she also wasn't sure she wanted to hear them. Had he hinted that perhaps it was her? No matter how badly her heart wanted to hear those words, she could not give in to whatever may be taking over her. As though to protect herself, she defiantly said,

"Matters of the heart are very different for you and me. A man of your rank has far more freedom of heart and evidently time than someone in my position."

Keeping his gaze on the fire, he said, "You are no better than me, Elizabeth. I know what you've seen." All the air in the space between them caught in the back of her throat. She couldn't speak. "Yes, Elizabeth, I know about your curiosities. And once I discovered your little secret, I ensured I never missed a Thursday with her, just in case you came back. And you almost always did."

She felt all the blood rush to her cheeks. What could she say?

What could she do? She wanted to deny it, to apologize, to run. He had turned toward her, eyes ablaze. She started to stand, but he pulled her arm to keep her seated in the chair. His gaze was locked with hers. He rose upon his knees and faced her in the chair. Slowly, she felt him pulling her closer until his lips were to her ear.

"I can make you feel that way, Elizabeth. I can give you more than you saw or can even imagine." She felt her knees weaken and her shoulders drop into his firm chest ever so slightly. He leaned down and brushed his lips across the back of her fingers. "I can make you feel things you have never felt." He kissed her fingers again, this time opening her palm. "I can show you things you never could imagine."

Kissing her palm now, he looked deeply into her eyes. She held his gaze, mesmerized at what was taking over her body, her consciousness, her reason. She closed her eyes as his lips traveled away from her wrist and to her elbow. He pulled her shift away just slightly to expose her skin. He let his lips trail up her collarbone to her neck, and she was delirious. So many thoughts were swarming in her head, and yet she couldn't make out anything, in particular, other than aching to know where the next kiss may land. Reaching her jawline, he pulled back, grasping her face gently between both hands, kissing her forehead, and whispering gruffly,

"I can't go further without you saying yes."

Her eyes opened at this pause, and she saw the window she had spent so many afternoons peering through. Perhaps it was the reality of getting caught by another onlooker or the immorality of what she was allowing herself to succumb to, but she quickly pushed herself from him, shaking her head and saying,

"I cannot. I cannot." Saying this over and over while she rushed to grab her clothes, which were still damp from the ride, she looked at him with near insanity in her eyes and said, "I will not!"

But she didn't have to tell him that. He had already backed away, standing aside as she scurried into her clothes. Finally, with her clothes back on, she looked at him with a gaze laced with fury, longing, and desperation.

"I'm sorry, Gregory."

"For what?" he asked hoarsely.

"For...for everything." And she turned and left as quietly as possible.

...

The weeks before Christmas passed quietly around the house. The earl had determined that he would use the entire month of December leading up to Christmas to gather his strength for what would be the most joyous Christmas yet. His daughters would all be in residence for the holidays, having returned from London to visit their father. And he had resumed his efforts to make a child with Elizabeth in mid-November, so he seemed optimistic that a son may yet be in his future.

Bitterly, Elizabeth thought how the moment she returned to the house after leaving Gregory's cottage in a hurry, she had a message from the earl that she should visit him that night. Not wanting to appear out of sorts, she did her best to encourage him. At one point, she even tried to moan as though she was enjoying it, but he quickly quieted her, saying it was interrupting his concentration. She let him thrust into her in silence. The only noise was his fleshy body slapping up against her thighs, and his groan when he finally reached his climax. She tried to will his seed into her womb as he collapsed on top of her.

But when her courses came the week before Christmas, she decided to feign illness so as not to ruin his jovial holiday spirit. Sadly, he took this as an encouraging sign, which made Elizabeth feel even more guilty, but she didn't want to let him down or have to start visiting his bed so soon.

Elizabeth overheard him telling one of his daughters that she was very fragile right now as they walked out of the dining hall and into the drawing room. She felt that was the best way to describe her the past few weeks—completely fragile, as though a light breeze would shatter her into a million pieces.

She tried not to think of Gregory, but forcing herself into

isolation left her with only her thoughts. What would have happened if she had said yes? Would she still feel as badly as she did now or worse? And if she had done it once, would she have been able to stop?

...

On Christmas Eve, Elizabeth woke with the sun to prepare for a day full of events and festivities. The earl's family always attended a Christmas Eve service with the entire staff at the local parish, followed by a luncheon and a gift-giving ceremony. Traditionally, the earl and countess gave each staff member a gift. Sometimes, they might receive a small gift in return.

Elizabeth chose a dark green dress with a fur stole to cover her arms. She planned to wear a matching green hat for the church service and then have her maid remove her pins to let her hair down for the gift ceremony. Catching her image in a mirror as she headed to the carriage, she noticed how gaunt her face had become. She barely recognized the woman she used to see in the mirror just a month before. Climbing into the carriage, the earl grabbed her hand instantly as they lurched forward down the drive and remarked how well she looked. Clearly, he didn't really see her, she thought.

"It is so good to see you well again, my dear Elizabeth," he said kindly as the carriage lurched into motion. "While I never want to wish you ill, it does give me hope for our son."

Elizabeth gently took his hand and said, "It is my sincerest hope that I will one day give you a son." He looked at her, his head slightly tilted. Then, to answer his unasked question, she said, "It will be my biggest prayer in today's service that we shall have a son by this time next year." Reading between the lines, the earl dropped his hand and, looking defeated, shook his head.

"I'm sorry, my dear. How hard this must be on you, too. Of course, my time is so much shorter, so I feel it more keenly, I know, but I am sure you must be devastated."

Trying to match his tone, Elizabeth said, "I want nothing more for us, John."

Then, the earl said with a bit of a laugh, "I must admit I am so desperate it would be just as well that you would get with child from another man just so I could die knowing that a son took over the title my family has held since the dissolution of the monasteries."

"You can't mean that. Of course you want a son of your own stock, and we will keep trying."

"I must admit, my little pet, that I have lost faith. I have never felt better than this last month, and yet it did not take." The two sat in silence as the carriage rocked subtly over the gravel of the long drive to the church.

"I'm serious, Elizabeth. If it would not sit too unwell with you, I can understand how a girl your age might like to try...else-where." Then, looking out the window for a while, clearly avoiding her gaze, he said in almost a whisper, "You wouldn't have to tell me."

Elizabeth just stared at him, mouth slightly agape, unsure she was hearing him clearly. Her mind was running with possibilities, and then, to make her stance on the matter clear, she said firmly, "You may have given up hope, John, but I have not. Pray for a son today, and we will do everything in our power to make him."

He looked at her with watery eyes and kissed her hand. The Earl wasn't an emotional, soft person, but at that moment, she knew that his tears were not due to her commitment to him but rather to the loss of the son, who would never be his.

...

The stone church was full of the earl's staff and the villagers by the time the countess and earl arrived. They walked down the aisle arm in arm so she could support him over the uneven stone floor. Elizabeth dared not to look around her for fear she may see Gregory. Throughout the whole service, the back of her neck prickled with the thought that he might be staring at her. But when they left the church, she did not find him in the crowd. Nor did she see him in their large dining room for the Christmas luncheon. As the minutes passed without spotting him, her mind began to play out a scene where he was with the laundress instead of at the Christmas celebration. Or worse, that he had left the estate altogether. But she was sure she would have heard of his departure if he had indeed decided to leave his position.

Feeling lightheaded and faint, Elizabeth told one of the earl's daughters she thought she would lie down for a moment. But before she could leave the crowd, she heard the butler announce that it was time for the gift-giving ceremony in the front hall. Knowing full well she had to be present, she told herself to stop thinking of him and tried to focus on her duty. Holding her head a little higher, Elizabeth strode through the hall into the foyer to take her place in a chair next to John. It was usually custom that they would stand to administer the gifts, but with John's fragile condition, the two thankfully could sit.

Elizabeth always enjoyed this part of the Christmas tradition. She loved giving gifts to those who served their house so well. But she equally enjoyed the few gifts they were given in return, as she knew so much thought and effort went into these tokens. This year, she received several gifts of embroidery, delicious biscuits, and dried bouquets from summer wildflowers. During their first year of marriage, Elizabeth was given several beautiful hand-embroidered baby items, but for the past two years, she has received nothing of the sort.

Seeing that the line had dwindled, she took a few extra moments to ask one of the young maids about the flowers in the dried bouquet she had been given. Impressed by the girl's knowledge of the local foliage, she told her about a book she would like to lend her that she had come across in the library over the summer. Consumed in this conversation, Elizabeth was not paying attention when the next group came forward to receive their gifts.

The earl tapped her on the arm and said, "Darling, your attention is required."

She smiled and told the girl how she would give the book to her maid and then turned back to the rest of the group. There standing before her husband were the stablemen, with Gregory at the forefront. She had never seen him outside the stables, so she was at a loss for words when she saw him in what she assumed were his best clothes with his hair pulled away from his face. He was here.

Gregory acknowledged the earl and the countess with a slight bow of his head. The earl gave them each a gift of new riding blankets for their horses and asked after his own horse whom he had not seen in months. The young men thanked him profusely and then moved on, but Gregory stopped in front of her and reached into his jacket pocket to pull out a small white figure.

"A Christmas token from your horse, Countess," he said.

She reached out and grasped the figure from his hands. It was a small doll made out of horsehair, just like he used to make his sisters. No doubt it was Majesty's hair. She looked up at him, at a complete loss of words, only to nod and finally say, "Thank you," in what was barely an audible whisper.

...

As the Christmas Eve festivities wore on with only the family and a few special guests remaining, Elizabeth did her very best to maintain her role as hostess. All through dinner, she played her part well, and seeing that her husband was getting particularly weary, she encouraged everyone to continue their celebrations in the library with music from the daughters. However, she said that she and the earl would be retiring early, and she could see how grateful he was for this interference.

"My dear, as much as I would love to have you share my bed, I am afraid I have no stamina tonight. We should enjoy one another tomorrow on Christmas Day." And with that, he kissed her cheek gruffly and went into his room, shouting out for his valet, who was only a few footsteps behind.

Closing herself into her own room, she immediately reached into her bodice to extract the doll from Gregory. She stroked it gently and then smelled it. It gave off a combination of woodsmoke and the oils from her horse. It flooded her with sadness, joy, desire, and longing. Then, she heard John's words echo in her mind. *"You wouldn't have to tell me."*

Making up her mind in an instant, she removed her silk shoes, pulled on her riding boots, and placed her riding cloak over her shoulders. Knowing that their guests would be noisily enjoying one another's company in the library and the household staff would be having Christmas dinner in the kitchens, she slipped down the front stairs and stole down the servant's hallway to one of the unmanned exits at the back of the house.

She had always been afraid of the dark, but as she walked quickly across the grounds without a lantern, her racing heart was not because of fear of the dark but fear of what she was doing. Finally coming to the stables lit by only a few lanterns, she heard raucous laughter and song from the far end. Several men and a few women were sharing ale and singing along to a violin. Having made no plans for what she would do once she arrived at the stable, she walked to Majesty's stall. She needed to catch her breath and buy herself time.

"Hello, my beauty," she whispered to the mare as she walked over and nuzzled her chest. Elizabeth stroked the side of her head through the fence and whispered, "I've missed you." And she had. Desperately. Staying away from Gregory had been devastating, but not seeing Majesty was almost just as hard in many ways. She had needed her more than ever this past month, but yet she couldn't bring herself to come back. Lost in the moment with her horse, she did not hear the footsteps from behind her.

"Elizabeth."

Closing her eyes to savor the sound of her name in his voice, she slowly turned. He was standing in the doorway to the stables wearing the same outfit from the gift ceremony. He was beautiful. Elizabeth wanted to touch and release the wavy hair he had pulled away from his face. She wanted to feel his hardened hands on her skin. She wanted to smell the woodsmoke on his clothes. He started walking towards her.

Trying to find the right words and to feel more confident than she did, she finally settled on, "I came to wish Majesty a happy Christmas." But her eyes told him everything that her mouth did not. She started walking towards him and then, stopping, she said, "I also wanted to thank you for the gift. It meant..." her voice caught in her throat. "It means everything to me." She looked up into Gregory's eyes, feeling her own moisten with the emotions taking over her.

"I've missed you," he whispered.

"I've missed you, too," she whispered back. And without thinking, without caring if she was spotted by the revelers, she grasped his hand and pulled him slowly out of the stables and into the night. Stopping in the middle of the frosty pasture, she whispered to him under the stars, "Yes."

And knowing exactly what she meant, he swept her into his arms and carried her to his cottage.

Gregory carried her through the door and sat her down gently on the table, kissing the top of her head. Then he went to add more wood to the fire and stoke it. Once it was crackling and casting an orange hue across the room, he returned to Elizabeth and held her face in his warm hands. She closed her eyes, willing herself to memorize this feeling of being held so gently.

"I've missed you, Elizabeth," he said again, and this time he kissed her on her lips, still holding her face.

She placed her hands on his hips. Their kisses were soft and gentle at first, but as their bodies pressed closer, the kisses became harder and more urgent. Gregory started unclasping her pelisse and then removed his own jacket down to his shirt-sleeves. Elizabeth let her hands trail up from his waist to feel his hardened muscles. She then tugged his shirt from his breeches and let her soft hands move up his sides to his back. He was warm, and his skin was soft and tight beneath her touch. She heard him take in a sharp breath as she started trailing her hands down his stomach to rest once again on his waist. Noticing how he responded to that touch, she moved her hands up and down his abdomen once again, and this time he let out a groan.

"You are wicked," he said, and she couldn't help but smile at his obvious enjoyment of the sensitive spots she had stumbled upon. She had never so much as touched her husband's skin, as they only ever copulated in their dressing gowns, or if he was feeling particularly energetic, he would just lift up her skirts.

As she went to do it again, Gregory stepped back and smiled devilishly, saying, "Your turn."

And with expert hands, he started slowly undressing her. She began to twist, trying to help him relieve her of her clothes more quickly, but he was taking impossibly long to undo the back of her gown. And by the time he got halfway down her back, he stopped and started trailing his fingers up and down her spine. She placed her forehead on his chest, savoring the feeling of his warm fingertips gently brushing her skin. Then he moved his hands to her shoulders and began slowly dropping her sleeves and lowering the front of her bodice to nearly reveal her breasts. But stopping just before her nipples could escape the fabric, he traced his fingers along the edge, following the slight swell of each breast. She yearned for him to pull it down further to see if it would relieve her of the mounting discomfort that was causing her to squirm.

Then as he finally pulled her gown down to her stomach, she gasped at the relief of having her breasts exposed. She watched Gregory's face as he looked at her breasts, her nipples hardening with the brush of air against her warm skin. Gently, he grazed a thumb around one nipple, causing it to harden more against his touch. He traced the same pattern around her other nipple and then slowly laid her back on the table so he could follow the path his fingertips made with his lips. Elizabeth could feel him breathe in her scent deeply as he traced his kisses up her neck and back to her mouth. The weight of him on her was making her even more breathless, and yet she found herself pulling him onto her harder, yearning for more.

And, as if he read her mind, she felt his hands lift her skirts to her thighs, and slowly, he started removing her riding boots and stockings. Now, a different feeling was competing with her desire, for she began to feel nervous. John had never once looked at her naked body, as though it wasn't a requirement for his mission. But now, as Gregory was looking at every inch of her body that he was touching, she started wondering what he would think when he saw her womanhood. Even Elizabeth had never seen herself fully. Yet she wanted him to look at her despite her nerves about what he would think. She found herself desperate for the comfort of his approval.

And so, to encourage herself to go on, she tugged her skirts up more, and to her surprise, she felt his warm lips on her inner thigh by her knee. Together, they lifted her skirts up to her abdomen. There she lay fully exposed to him. She waited anxiously for some sort of response, and when his lips finally trailed to nearly between her legs, he drew back and looked at her in the firelight.

"My God, Elizabeth, you are beautiful."

And, as if to confirm his words, he leaned back down, buried his face in the soft brown hair between her legs, and breathed in deeply. Losing control of herself, she felt her hips thrust toward his face as if trying to pull it down between her legs. Reading her desire, he kissed her right on the soft, hairless skin of her womanhood. The sensation was more than she could handle, but he kissed her again, and again, and again. She reached to hold the back of his head to encourage him to do it more, but when he started kissing her more deeply, she groaned with overwhelming pleasure and pulled his head away. She couldn't take what was building up inside her, nor did she know how to relieve it.

Standing over her, Gregory started unlacing his breeches. But before pulling them down, he said gruffly, "This is where you have to tell me to stop, Elizabeth. Because once we start, you can never undo what we are about to do." And after a pause, he added, "I don't want you to regret anything."

She sat up and, holding his cheek, whispered in his ear, "The only thing I will ever regret with you is running away last time."

And to prove her confidence in her decision, she started to lower his breeches. His manhood lurched out of them immediately, finally freed from the constraints of the fabric. Elizabeth stared at him, shocked by how firm and straight his manhood was. She had only caught glances at her husband's as she felt it might be indecent of her to look at him.

Slowly, she reached up to brush her fingers along the coarse, dark mass of hair encircling him. Then she brushed the back of her fingers along the length of his manhood. He groaned, arching his neck as he looked up toward the ceiling. She was surprised at how soft the skin was and could feel the pulsing within it. She then placed her whole hand around him and stroked him again, feeling his knees give. She stopped, worried that she had done something wrong. But quickly, he grabbed her hand and guided her so that she moved back and forth along him, encouraging her with more groans of pleasure.

Delighted by her ability to weaken him, she used her free hand to pull his face towards hers, and she started kissing him. But he couldn't match her kisses due to his panting. She knew from her limited past experience that his pleasure was mounting, and he obviously knew it, too, as he pulled himself away from her grasp.

"I have to have you," he said. And Elizabeth knew exactly how he was feeling because she had the same force of desire pulsing between her own legs. She started to lay back down on the table, but Gregory lifted her up and instead carried her to the chair by the fire—the very chair she had sat in when she had been caught in the rainstorm and had desperately wanted what she was finally now giving herself. He sat down with her on top of him, her skirts smashed between them.

"I want you to take your pleasure from me, Elizabeth, however you want it." Elizabeth had no idea what he meant, but she started kissing him anyway, knowing that her body and Gregory would guide her. He pulled back from her lips and stuck two of his fingers in his mouth. Then, he reached between them and touched her between her legs. She could tell that she was wet with desire, and he smiled, saying breathlessly, "You obviously didn't need me to do that."

He then lifted her onto the top of him, and with his strength, he slowly placed his manhood at her entrance. Elizabeth found herself slowly lowering onto him, the pressure of his manhood opening her in the most delicious way. Both of their mouths were agape at the sensations they were experiencing. Lowered entirely on top of him, she placed her head on his shoulder and let their bodies be together. Breathing as one, she nuzzled into his neck, and he slowly stroked her bare back down to her skirts.

When her husband had pushed into her, it had always felt so intrusive, but with Gregory in her, she could feel her body welcoming him, the muscles almost pulling him into her. And, as if following her body's cues, she started rocking against him. The tickle of his hair against her was the most delicious sensation, causing her body to yearn for more. Gregory took his hands off her back and held onto the arms of the chair, his knuckles white from his firm grip. Feeling the desire build within her, she slowly raised herself up him and then back down. Over and over, she did this, mixed in with rocking herself onto him.

Their breathing stayed as one with the slow rhythmic moving of her hips. But, as she started to move faster, Gregory let out a deep groan and moved his hand from the chair to between her legs. He pressed his fingers against the soft, silky part of her womanhood, and he held her there as she continued to move up and down him. A moan escaped her mouth as the pleasure began to escalate. She felt out of control with the force overtaking her. Still, even though she was near some sort of oblivion, she was also very aware of Gregory and the near desperation that had taken over his movements.

Moving faster, she felt a warmth overtake the inside of her body, followed by the most delectable, ecstatic release. Her body pulsed against him as if pulling him further into her. And amidst her own oblivion, she felt him release inside her with such a force that all strength seemed to leave her tired body. She melted into him.

With the fire dancing behind them in the grate, Gregory and Elizabeth sat together as one until their breathing finally slowed, and he began to soften inside her. Pushing off reality for as long as she could, she nuzzled even closer to him and whispered, "Thank you."

Stroking her hair, he whispered back, "Thank you, Elizabeth."

...

The earl never fully recovered from whatever overtook him on Christmas Eve. His daughters attributed it to too much exertion over hosting a most wonderful Christmas party, but Elizabeth knew better. She knew that it was the defeat of knowing he would never have a son of his own. It was what happened to a person when they had finally given up all hope in attaining what they wanted most in life.

Elizabeth remained devoted to the earl's bedside through the remainder of that winter and early spring of 1808. She fed him when he would take food, rubbed his arms and legs to help him relax, and ensured he had regular doses of laudanum to keep him comfortable when he was fearful or anxious. Being in the same room as a person waiting for death while you so desperately wanted to cling to life is a most impossible place.

Her only refuge was riding Majesty in the afternoons when the earl was sure to be asleep. Perhaps it was guilt for what she had done and continued to do, but Elizabeth only gave herself an hour or two at most away from his bedside during the day.

Her belly swelled with child as the daffodils began to blossom, and Elizabeth grappled with whether or not to tell her husband about the child growing in her. But seeing that he was hanging on for something, she finally told him one day when he seemed remarkably calm. When the news reached his ears, he looked at her with his clear grey eyes and beckoned her to come toward him. She placed his hand on her swelling belly and said,

"I never had my courses at Christmastime. The doctor predicts he should be born in the autumn."

He sat up in bed with what strength he had and, still holding her belly, he said, "What incredible news, my pet. What incredible news. You will name him John for me and for my father and grandfather, yes?" She saw the pleading in his eyes.

"Exactly what I was thinking myself."

"How I wish I would meet him," he said sadly but still with

a smile on his face. And knowing that it was unlikely he ever would, Elizabeth just sat on the bed next to him and let him rest his hand on her belly until he finally was sleeping again. Weeks later, the Earl of Lincolnshire passed, leaving his entire estate to his young wife and his heir she was carrying.

...

As the leaves began to turn and the misty rains took residence over England for what would be the next several months, Elizabeth gave birth to a healthy baby.

"What shall we call her?" Gregory asked Elizabeth once all her attendants and the physician had left so he could finally sneak in to meet his daughter.

"Penny," she said.

Gregory smiled. "Penny," he said, trying it out. "She's perfect. Just like her mother." And he bent to kiss both of them.

Newly widowed and in control of the estate that her daughter would eventually inherit due to her late husband's will, Elizabeth was finally free to be the woman she wanted to be and to marry if she chose. And, of course, she did. She and Gregory went on to have several more children, all of whom looked suspiciously like the earl's daughter, Penny.

But no one said anything.

2

Margary's Story

It's Yule in the year 1199.

Richard The Lionheart's army is returning from The Third Crusade after the king fell on the battlefield in France. One of his prized archers, Edric, son of Everard of Lancaster, has finally returned home.

His wife, Margary, whom he married when they were sixteen, has spent their ten years of marriage in his parents' home. Having no news of home for the past four years, he did not know what or who to expect upon his return. And Margary had no idea if her husband was even alive.

During this Yule season, she is trying to ensure her mother-in-law has a warm fire, the children of the village have bread and honey, and the animals are safe from thieves for another night.

"Are you warm enough, Joan?" Margary asked, tucking the blanket tightly around the old woman's legs. The fire was spitting out sparks as she made her final tucks.

"Yes, yes, I am fine, dear," her mother-in-law replied meekly. Margary turned back to move several smaller logs in front of the fire so the woman could roll them with her walking stick should she get chilled later in the night.

"I will come to you first thing in the morning. Bragge will stay with you and keep you company." The old woman looked at her intently.

"You are not sleeping out in the barn again, are you, Margary?" she asked gruffly. Margary started busying herself by fluffing up the straw bed for the dog that was to keep watch that night.

"Margary?" she said more loudly this time.

Margary sighed. "It is no problem. You shouldn't worry about me at all. It's plenty warm in the straw, and I have a good blanket with me."

"And what if you do catch the thief?" Joan asked quizzically.

"Then I shall rest much easier tomorrow night, knowing that he will no longer be our concern," she said with more confidence than she felt.

"This shouldn't be your burden. Edric should be here. Fighting his own battles at home."

"But alas, he is not, Joan, and he has not been for some ten years. We fight on without him." The old woman huffed, but Margary pressed on. "I promise, tonight will be the last night I sleep outside. Once Yule has passed, I imagine the thief will feel less desperate and will likely move on to other parts of the county when he realizes nothing is left here for taking."

And with that, Margary bent down to kiss her mother-in-law's head and bid her goodnight. Bragge quickly jumped up to trail after her as she walked out the door.

"Not tonight, Bragge," she said to the dog. "You stay with Joan." The dog stood in the doorway as she descended the stairs into the house's main hall, and she heard him patter back to where he was supposed to pass his night.

Before heading to the barn, Margary walked to the kitchen and rinsed her face with a cool jug of water left for her by Amabel, their cook. The few staff they had were relieved of their duties for the evening as there was a Yuletide gathering at the mead hall. Knowing full well that revelry could serve as the perfect distraction for most townsfolk and leave them vulnerable to thieves, Margary took extra care to get to the barn quickly that night.

Expecting it to be especially cold as snow was dusting the courtyard, Margary grabbed an extra blanket and wrapped a fur around her shoulders. Heading into the barn, she closed the gate behind her, taking care to leave a metal pail filled with rocks on the other side so it would clang if someone tried to open it. And, as she did every night for the past two months, she tied up their only miking cow onto a post with a bell attached. Then she prepared her bed of straw in a shadowy corner so she had a perfect position to ambush any thieves. Settling in, she welcomed the barn cat, heavy with kittens, under her covers.

"Any day now," Margary whispered to the purring feline as she kneaded her paws into the blanket beneath them. "You can come inside with me to keep your little ones safe."

She would give anything to feel safe herself. The failed harvest had made for desperate people in the county. Unrelenting rains all throughout the fall had soured the crops. Fortunately, because most of the able-bodied men were either still fighting in the crusade or dead on the battlefield, there were fewer mouths to feed. But women, children, and the elderly were hungry. The boys who were too young to fight in the most recent campaign turned to thievery, as did the men who were released from jail because the jailers, too, were sent abroad. It wasn't the young boys she feared. She knew they would flee the moment they saw her if they were caught trying to steal her milk cow. It was the former prisoners

—the men who already were tainted and wouldn't think twice about killing her cow, or her, for that matter.

Despite the very sincere threat of thieves, Margary was exhausted from preparing for Yule and felt the heaviness of sleep slowly overtake her. She knew she had to be up early to help ready the fresh loaves for the hungry village children anticipating bread and honey on Christmas Day. Margary had started the tradition in years past when bread was aplenty. But now, it was all she could do to keep bread on the table for her household. Just before giving way to sleep, she felt for her knife in its sheath around her right calf. She kept her hand on it while curled around the cat, ready to strike if necessary.

...

Margary woke to the sound of hooves in the courtyard. It felt like only moments later. Her heart was pounding instantly, making it hard to hear anything over the fear coursing through her veins. She pulled the knife out slowly and waited.

The hooves stopped just outside the gate to the barn. She heard boots hit the dirt. The rider had obviously dismounted, and it sounded as though there was only one. At least there wasn't a group of them, she thought. Margary sprung up from her nest in the straw and slunk against the wall. The thief was now at the gate, and she heard the rusted hinges start squealing as it began to open. The gate hit the metal bucket, which made a loud clang, causing the hens to rustle and cluck on their perches. She could not let him get through the gate. It was now or never.

"There is nothing here for you but certain death," she said in a deep, threatening voice. The thief paused at the gate.

"I have faced death for thousands of days," the thief said in a quiet, hollow voice. It sent chills up Margary's spine.

"There is nothing for you here," Margary replied coldly. "Leave, or you will die."

"Everything I have is here," he replied. "Or was."

Margary stopped breathing. Her mind was racing. Was it a trap? Or was it *him*? Finding strength from somewhere deep within, she rounded the corner and stepped into the moonlight from the shadows of the barn, knife gripped in her fist. They stared at each other. He looked so unfamiliar, and yet, she would know those eyes anywhere.

"Margary," he whispered. She just looked at him, taking him in. He was bigger than she remembered. He had always been tall, but he had also been so lanky. Even beneath the layers of chainmail, leather, and fur keeping him warm, she could tell he had hardened from his years abroad. And he had grown a beard. The moonlight was likely deceiving, but he looked so much older in his face.

"Edric?" she said, finally finding her voice. He nodded. Her husband had returned. A flood of confusing emotions coursed through her veins. Anger. Heartbreak. Fear. Sadness. She kept her feet firmly in place.

"Surprised to see me?" he asked, still softly.

"I thought you were dead."

"There were many times I also thought I was dead."

Margary looked around the barn, not knowing what to say.

"Are you well?" he inquired.

"You're asking me if I am well?" she asked, exasperated. "I haven't heard from you in two years. No letter. No news from any other returning soldiers. And now you are here? No, I am not well!" He looked taken aback.

"I shouldn't have come like this. I just couldn't wait to be...to be home."

Margary shuffled her feet, and then, not knowing what to do with her hands, she lifted her skirts and sheathed the knife back into its holster on her calf.

"Were you going to kill me?" he asked, surprised.

"You have no idea what I have had to do in your absence," Margary said darkly. She then moved the metal bucket with some effort and opened the gate.

"Bring your horse in. There's an unused stall where your father's horse was kept."

"Is Father gone?"

Margary nodded and said, "He died last winter from fever. I think he gave up hope you would ever be home. We had to sell off his horse this fall to survive. The harvest failed."

After she said all of this, she realized that she could have been gentler in sharing this news with him. Edric had been close to Everard. He brought his horse into the stall and was quiet for some time.

"And Mother?" he asked, somewhat hesitantly.

"She is alive—very feeble. And quite fragile since your father's death. Her mind is not well anymore, either. She gets confused easily."

He nodded again, then lifted off the gear he brought on his horse. Meanwhile, Margary carried in fresh hay and broke a thin layer of ice that had formed on the top of the water bucket so the horse could drink. Edric threw a wool blanket over the horse's back, and the two stepped out of the stall. When they bumped into one another as they went through the dark, Margary felt like she was with a complete stranger.

"There likely is still a fire going in the kitchens if you want to go warm up in there. You will find bread, meats, and ale on the table. The staff is out to celebrate Yule, so you won't be disturbed. I recommend you sleep in the kitchens so as not to disturb your mother or alarm Bragge."

"Bragge?"

"He's a stray that wandered into our lives about five years ago. He's a good watchdog."

"Then why is he not here in your stead?"

"Because he is watching over your mother. It makes me feel better knowing he is there when I'm here where I can't hear her call for me."

Margary was walking back to her nest in the hay when Edric reached out for her arm.

"I will sleep here. You go inside and keep warm."

"Nonsense. You must be exhausted. I am perfectly fine outside."

"I insist. I am in no state to be in the house, anyway." Margary knew what he meant. He was in need of a bath, as she could smell the sweat, smoke, and horse oil even several feet away from him.

"Fine," she said. "You are right. You need to wash. I shall have the water warmed first thing in the morning." Before she walked out, she added, "Please let the cat sleep with you. She has grown accustomed to me sleeping in here with her."

Edric nodded, looking over toward the grey feline with her large belly. He had never taken to cats, as Margary slyly knew, but he was so tired he wouldn't argue with her now.

"Good night, Margary," he said.

"Good night," she replied, somewhat more sharply than she intended. Why was she so angry? She had hoped for this moment for ten years—from the second she knew he would be leaving on the crusade. What had changed? *Time*, she thought bitterly to herself. She had lost her youth, her idealism, her romantic view of the world as she had known it. Spending the last ten years trying to run the largest farm in the village and having the weight of so many people depending on them aged her more than a decade. She had entered her marriage young, naive, and excited for a future with Edric. But all that had fallen away with the years he was gone.

As she tucked herself deep into her cold bed—their old bed— she tried to recall how he had felt when they were first married.

They had fallen hard and quickly for one another, and despite his parents wishing him to marry higher, Edric proposed marriage to her within a few weeks of his first venture into the forest with her and her sisters.

Margary grew up in the neighboring village and was the oldest of three sisters. Edric had a band of boys he was always with —they were inseparable. They made decisions as a unit, which at one time had been fun and innocent. But, when the rest of them decided to join King Richard's crusade, Edric was pulled between being a newly married man and seeking what glory may lie in battle.

Margary could still feel the sobs wracking her body as she begged Edric not to go and the anger she felt as she threw her wedding ring made of thread at him. But even though they hadn't courted long, she knew him so well and hated him for his loyalty to his friends. He was by far the best swordsman and archer in their group, and he wouldn't let them fight alone.

Knowing that the last time they parted, she had felt betrayed by him and trapped in a life that was not hers, she couldn't wrap herself around who she was supposed to be to him anymore. A loving wife surely didn't feel right, yet she couldn't deny the pull in her stomach toward him the moment she recognized him tonight. Would he feel the same if they ever touched again? Did his heart still belong to her after all these years, or had he found comfort in another's arms? She was in no position to blame him if he had. When she finally gave in to sleep, Margary had the deepest, most restful sleep she had in years.

...

When she awoke the following day, sunlight was streaming through the small window in her bedchamber. The yellow glow in the room was absolutely still and beautiful. She had never seen it like this—well, not in a long time. Not since they were first married. She remembered that light well, in fact. How it would dance on the sheets while they made love in those early days; how they would not go downstairs until the sun was high in the sky when guilt for not giving his father a hand early in the morning finally forced him out of bed.

Margary stretched fully, her bare arms reaching up toward the canopied bed. It felt surprisingly warm for this time of year. Unusually warm. Sitting up, she saw a fire had been lit in the hearth. She hadn't had a fire in weeks. The staff wouldn't have thought she was here in the first place, and they didn't have extra wood chopped for more than the kitchen fire and Joan's room. It must have been Edric, she thought.

Quickly, she got out of bed and put on a clean dress for the morning Christmas festivities. She had told him she would have the water warming for a bath first thing, and she had to get ready to deliver fresh loaves of bread to the children. Then, she was to play hostess to several of the more prominent members of the village, including the local sheriff, the priest, the commissioner, and several neighbors. How glad she was for so many distractions so she wouldn't have to deal with her emotions.

Rushing downstairs, she headed straight for the kitchens to see if Amabel had readied the baskets for her. But when she walked into the open kitchen, the table was full of the food for the evening supper.

"Where are the loaves, Amabel?" she asked breathlessly.

"The master already loaded the cart and is delivering them now. Can you believe he is back? And with such timing as to be here for Yule. Ye must be so thrilled, madam," Amabel said kindly. "Of course, we had all given up hope. Such a blessing."

"Yes, indeed. I am still trying to process it myself," Margary replied slowly. "Do you know how long it has been since he left?"

"It was just after daybreak, madam. He went to see his mother first thing—taking her some hot mulled wine. The mistress has been in fits all morning since he left. Says she can't believe he is back. Keeps calling him Everard, though, poor lady."

Margary nodded. She was afraid that his homecoming might throw Joan off completely.

"Do you need anything from me before I head into the village?" Margary asked.

"Nay, madam. Just sent my lass to gather eggs. Should be able to put something together nicely for your gathering tonight, madam."

"Thank you, Amabel. Whatever would I do without you?" Margary said sincerely.

"Let's hope ye never have to find out," she said with a smile, turning back to her chopping at the large wooden table that dominated much of the kitchen space.

Margary went back upstairs to check in on Joan but found her sleeping soundly when she approached. Adjusting her blanket, Margary left the withered woman to rest and returned downstairs to throw on her cloak and boots. Then, she headed out to ready her horse for the short trip to the village.

The ride was cold, with frost still on the ground from the dusting of snow that had fallen overnight. From the clouds in the distance, it looked like more would be headed their way that night.

Coming into the small village, Margary saw a small gathering just outside the church with a fire lit in the center of the gathering. Children were playing with hoops and swords carved from branches. Dogs were slinking around the gathering, looking for extra bits of scraps that may have fallen. Margary saw the crowd assembled around her cart, which she had only put festive greenery around yesterday. And there in the center stood Edric, taller than everyone save for the unusually tall vicar. She hopped down from her horse and watched him amongst the group. A small boy tugged at his sleeve, and in recognition, Edric bent down and gave him a chunk of bread wrapped in cloth. The boy ran off quickly to devour his bread before someone else took notice.

Several women appeared to be asking him questions, of which he seemed to take great care in answering. Probably wanting news of their own men, she thought to herself. But then another thought crept into her mind. Edric was one of the few men who had returned. Times had been unusually difficult, and Margary knew that the women were desperate for something to take their minds away from it. Being the only ones running what was left of their families' businesses, caring for the children and the elderly, and fending off thieves from stealing what little they had—Margary understood why Edric was such a ray of light for the women gathered there. He brought hope. And, now that she saw him in the light, he was incredibly strong and beautiful to look at as well.

Winding her way to his side, she caught his eye, and he stopped in the middle of what he was saying. The crowd of women followed his gaze, and they parted to let her through as she said, "Good morning, husband."

He broke into a careful smile, and she walked up to his side. Then Edric finished telling the crowd about how many of the men who served with King Richard in his final battle at the siege of Châlus were still in the capital waiting for their wages.

"And did ye get yours?" asked Beatrice, a gruff-looking woman with a handful of children weaving in and out of the crowd. Several women shuffled their feet, feeling the awkwardness of this question.

"No," said Edric firmly.

"The new King John doesn't pay then?" another woman asked loudly.

"Of course not!" Beatrice said harshly. "But 'e certainly expects us to pay 'im!"

Heads moved in agreement throughout the crowd. Along with the terrible harvest, taxation had also increased to an unmanageable level, and people were worried about how to survive the upcoming collection.

Edric held up his hand to calm the grumbling crowd. "The king may plan to pay soldiers' wages eventually or perhaps already has. I didn't stay long enough to find out."

"Why?" Beatrice asked.

"Because I wanted to get home," Edric said plainly.

"What good are ye if ye don't bring any money?" Beatrice

said, laughing harshly. "If me husband were to come home with empty pockets, I'd send 'im right back to war!"

But neither Edric nor Margary heard or at least acknowledged her because, as he said that, they met each other's eyes, and so much was said in that look. So much had been lost. And yet, there was still something. Margary could feel it. And she knew Edric could, too. Why else would his piercing blue eyes be looking at her that way? Margary broke eye contact first, fearing that her emotions would start pouring through her eyes.

...

The rest of the day passed slowly. Margary spent it in almost a dreamlike state. They wrapped up the cart after Edric had finished handing out the bread, sat together through the Christmas service, and rode slowly home with the cart in tow. Their talk was superficial at first—what happened with the harvest, who else had made it home, who was known to be dead, and more details of his father's last days. But then, he turned to her, asking,

"How did you manage, Margary?"

Swallowing hard and keeping her eyes focused on the road, she said, "I don't know. I suppose because that's all I could do. And, I always had hope...at least until the last year."

"What did you hope for?"

"That you would come home," she replied quietly. Feeling the tears collecting under her eyes but fighting hard to keep them back, she leaned down to pat her mare's head and urged her to walk just slightly ahead of his. Their decade apart had hardened a big part of her, yet his homecoming was completely breaking down the walls she had put up to keep herself safe.

"I promised you that I would." Margary couldn't reply immediately. She just kept her gaze hard ahead.

Finally arriving on their land, Margary dismounted, and Edric took her reins. She muttered that she needed to check how Amabel was getting on with the food and rushed off toward the house.

Everything had been set, and there was little to do. Margary added logs to the hearth in the dining chamber to get it plenty warm for her mother-in-law and then went upstairs to change into her finest dress. She took out her hair and brushed it. She hadn't worn it down in so long, but as she started pinning it back up, she thought better of it and left it cascading down her back. Edric had always said he loved her golden red hair and often played with the tendrils as he kissed her softly.

Sinking into her bed to put on fresh stockings, she stopped and stared at her bare fingers. About three years into their marriage, her wedding ring had fallen apart. Edric had made it out of wool thread—it was all he was able to give her at that time when they were so young. Even though she had thrown it at him, she slipped it back over her finger the moment he rode down the road away from their home and into war. Margary still kept what was left of the small strand next to her bedside. For several years, she had made bands out of threads that had come loose on her bedclothes, but she eventually stopped wearing anything on her finger altogether.

Now that he was back, she found herself playing with some thread that had come loose on the dress she had been wearing earlier. She wanted to weave it into a ring, but then it wouldn't be right to wear it, not after what she had done.

How was she going to tell him? She wouldn't have done what she did if she had even the slightest inclination that he might return. She had been desperate, heartbroken, empty, and lonely. And William had been so attentive to her. Margary would have never given herself to him, but she felt all was lost and was starting to think about what she would do when Joan died. Already, they had hardly any money, and supporting both women plus a minimal household was more than they could afford.

William was the sheriff of the town and a decent man. He had lost his wife in childbirth two years ago, and he and Margary had developed a friendship over their mutual losses. Margary never loved him, but she had grown to care for him. And she never would have married him until she had official word that Edric had died. Still, she had also felt she couldn't keep stringing him along without giving something of herself. And she cared so little for her physical self after Edric had left that to give herself to him didn't seem to affect her in any way—good or bad. Not until now—now that Edric was here and desire and guilt had been burning within her from the moment she saw him last night.

He would never forgive her. She was sure of it. But she had to tell him before William came over for dinner. She had no choice. Making up her mind to do it right away, she tossed the thread aside and headed downstairs.

Voices reached her ears the moment she stepped onto the landing. *No, not already.* She could hear Edric and the vicar talking. A third voice also chimed in, though she only heard it murmur a few pleasantries. William was already here. Drawing in a deep breath, Margary left the stairwell and entered the dining hall. All three men looked at her, the vicar instantly walking to greet her. She then turned to William. She could see the pain on his face as he only briefly nodded in her direction and then turned to greet the few remaining guests—neighbors who had just come through the front of the house.

Edric walked up beside her and said quietly, "You are beautiful, Margary." She looked longingly at him and imagined herself telling him that she needed to speak with him, but she knew they couldn't pull away from their guests, and she didn't want to upset the night just yet. She prayed under her breath that nothing would be spoiled until everyone left.

Prayers answered, the dinner went smoothly, and the

conversation was filled with Edric's stories of his travels. He spoke of the different people he saw, the vibrant textiles people wore, and the unique animals and terrain. But he never told of the fighting itself. At one point, John, their nearest neighbor, asked about Edric's friends' whereabouts.

"All dead," he replied softly. John shook his head, muttering what a shame it was. Margary knew that two of his group of six had died near the beginning of the journey—one in battle, the other from a wound sustained in a fight with another English soldier.

"What will you do now that you are home?" John's wife Matilda asked.

"Try to pick up the pieces here." Then, to lighten the mood, he laughed, "I will start by building a better fence to help my wife feel safer at night."

"You needn't have worried about her too much. Sheriff kept an awfully close eye on the place while you were away," John said kindly, raising his jug to William.

Margary held her breath, but Matilda spoke up rather quickly, saying, "We all have William to thank for keeping order around here."

"O' course! But William here gave extra special care to this property. Always asking us after Margary, wasn't he Matilda?"

"And Joan, too," Matilda said. Margary wondered if she had suspected anything between her and the Sheriff. Glancing at William quickly, she saw he was keeping his eyes on his plate. Margary felt Edric's gaze on her.

"I am grateful to everyone who helped look after my home and family."

...

The rest of the evening felt interminably long to Margary. Amabel had outdone herself with what little they had, making everyone's belly full of spiced bread to conclude the meal. With snow starting to fall, their guests finally departed into the crisp night, leaving Edric, Joan, and Margary by the fireside.

"William was quiet tonight," Joan observed.

"I don't know him. Is he a quiet man?" Edric replied.

"Not usually around here. He probably feels the loss of his wife and the loneliness, particularly around this time of year. And I am sure seeing you come home, Edric, while his wife will never come back, was hard."

"Mmm," Edric hummed. But he was looking at Margary.

Not knowing what to do with herself, she stood and said, "I never filled the bath for you. I will go heat the water."

"That's not necessary," Edric said.

But Joan replied quickly, "Nonsense! You smell like you brought the whole barn in with you. Couldn't you have washed before dinner?"

"I will take care of my own water, Margary," he called after her, but she pretended not to hear. "Shall I take you upstairs, Mother?"

"Not tonight, Edric. Often, I sleep in front of the fire here as it means Margary doesn't have to carry wood up to my room and start a fire."

"Well, I am here now. I will do it."

"You will not. Tonight, you need to focus on your wife. Bring me an extra fur and lay some straw down for Bragge. We will be just fine."

Edric did as he was told and then went to the kitchens to help haul buckets. Seeing two sitting aside the large cauldron over the fire, Edric poured the hot water into them and hoisted them up the staircase to their bedroom. When they were first married, Edric had built a solid wooden tub in front of their fire so Margary would have her own tub and would not have to share a bath with his parents. He shouldered the door open and found her draping the tub in a linen cloth.

He put down his buckets and helped her secure the cloth around the tub. Then, he added logs to the hearth and started the fire. Margary emptied the buckets and then slipped back down the stairwell for more. Edric followed her, bringing his buckets. Together, they made several trips until the tub was shoulder-level.

"There's soap next to some washing linen on the table, and here is a cloth to dry off," Margary said awkwardly, handing him a towel. And with that, she turned on her heel to leave the room, but he grabbed her arm.

"Margary." She felt her breath catch in her throat. "Why won't you look at me?" he asked, his eyes pleading with her. She just stared at the floor, unable to find the words. "I know we are different people than when I left. But I want to know you again. I am willing to do whatever it takes to help you come back to me. As my wife."

Margary looked at his strong, scarred hand clasped around her arm. Finding courage from somewhere deep inside her, she gently removed his hand from her arm and squared herself to him.

"I am not the woman you left ten years ago, Edric."

"I know that," he said, his frustration starting to mount, but she softly touched her finger to his lips.

"I need you to listen to me. This is already hard enough to say to you."

Edric stared at her, waiting. Swallowing hard, she tried to find the words but couldn't.

"You don't want to be my wife anymore," he said, unable to wait for the inevitable.

"Of course not. Being a wife to you and having you home was all I longed for, but Edric—" she paused, her heart pounding in her ears. "I lost hope that you would come home. And I made a terrible mistake. I was lonely and..." Silence, thick as smoke, hung in the air between them.

"You gave yourself to another man," Edric said simply.

Tears began to well up in Margary's eyes. She looked at him, trying to read his face, which had gone ghostly white. He walked over to the bed and nearly sat on it but thought better of it, given the state of his clothes. Sliding down to the floor, he rested his head in his hands.

"I never stopped loving you, Edric. But I stopped believing you would ever come home. I heard nothing from you for two years. And I was scared."

"Who is it?" he asked gruffly. Margary didn't answer. He took his hands off his face and looked at her. She expected him to be angry and to look at her with loathing, but he just looked...heartbroken.

"It was William, the sheriff. We both had lost our spouses—or so I thought." Edric nodded, looking at the ground.

"And did you give your heart away, along with the rest of you?"

"Of course not!" Margary said, her voice raised. She felt a tinge of anger that he had put it that way. She walked over to him and knelt on the floor before him.

"Edric, you won't be able to understand. I had to make plans so I was not toiling away at a farm that was never mine that you would never come home to. I couldn't afford to stay. You won't ever know how hard it has been, but I needed...I needed security."

"And did you not think what would happen if I did come home?"

"Every single day since it happened," she said quietly.

"How many times, Margary? How many times were you with him?"

"Twice," she said in a whisper. "It was after the harvest failed. I felt so defeated."

"So he took advantage of you then? Of your circumstance?" he said, his voice quivering with anger.

"No, Edric," she said. "I did so willingly."

"You are not the woman I thought you were, then," he said, getting back on his feet.

Margary stayed on the ground. And then, finding the fight in her, she stood and looked him squarely in the eyes.

"I am not the only one to blame, Edric. Lest we not forget, you choose to leave me."

Edric raised his head. "I *chose* to go?"

"Yes," she hissed back at him. "You chose your band of brothers over me. I will never forgive you for leaving me just weeks after we married. It was your choice to go with them—all of you hungry for riches and women. Oh yes, I heard them talking to you the week before you left. I know what they wanted. I just couldn't believe it was what you wanted, too," she said scathingly.

"I would have been forced into the army anyway, Margary!

Better that I chose to go of my own accord!" he shouted at her. Margary jumped back, alarmed by his raised voice. Good, she thought to herself. It was easier to have him angry than sad. "And how dare you attack my motives for going."

"Then why did you leave me, Edric? Why?" Margary shouted back.

"Because of loyalty, Margary!"

"Yes, loyalty to them, but not to me!"

"My loyalty to you has never faltered, Margary. I have remained a faithful husband to you these last ten years." She looked at him disbelievingly, which he did not fail to miss. "I never was with another woman while I was away, Margary. And yes, I have always been loyal to my friends, but my motive for going was not just to see them out alive and experience the world beyond this village. I went so that I could provide for you and the family I dreamed of having with you. Being children of farmers, you and I have always known what it is like to have the threat of hunger ever present in our minds. I did not want my children to know what that is like."

And then, as if to put the final nail in the coffin of her resolve, he said, "You are what kept me alive, Margary."

She couldn't suppress the tears any longer. For nearly ten years, she kept them at bay, believing that the moment she allowed one tear to fall, she would have lost all hope in him coming home. When the harvest failed, she'd sobbed and sobbed in the barn. Not only would there be little to feed anyone over the winter and spring, but she'd cried for Edric, for the future she dreamt of, for the woman she wanted to be. Rumors had spread widely by that point that the king had died in January, and all soldiers were back on Anglican soil. Some had even returned home to neighboring counties. Word hadn't reached her that most were waiting for payment. She had no choice but to assume he had died, for she knew he would have come home as soon as he was back.

It was in that state that William had found her in the barn, and he'd held her as she cried. Then, they'd cried together at both of their losses. Through all the emotions clawing their way out of both of them, she'd found herself lifting her dress to encourage the hand that had started traveling up her leg.

Tears starting to stream down her face, she said, "I thought you died, Edric. Even seeing you now, I am unsure if you are real or just a ghost haunting me for what I did."

Edric closed the space between them in one footstep, grabbed her hands gently, and put them on his chest. Margary started to cry harder, her legs weakening under the weight of it all.

"I am real," he whispered.

Slowly, she found herself falling into his arms, her cheek

pressed into the thick wool of his tunic. He reached up and started stroking her hair down her back. She could feel him nuzzle his nose into her hair, inhaling deeply. With his arms wrapped tightly around her, Margary lost all control and started sobbing. The pain had been so intense, and yet the more she wept, the better she began to feel. It was as though the harder she cried, the lighter everything became. Slowly, she felt herself relax into him, and they began to sway on the spot.

"I don't blame you," he said, still stroking her hair.

Margary shook her head and said into his chest, "I am so sorry, Edric."

But instead of letting her apology sit between them, he lifted her chin so that she was looking into his blue eyes, "I love you, Margary. I always will love you."

As they stared into one another's eyes a moment longer, Edric began slowly closing the distance between their faces, and their lips met in a whisper-soft kiss. Lingering for as long as possible, they kissed again, and then again with more urgency. Finding a rhythm to their kisses, they brought their hands on each other's faces, pulling them harder toward one another. Edric started drawing her closer to him by her hair while she ran her palm across the back of his neck. Breaking apart for but a moment, Edric quickly removed his boots and as he stood back up, he pulled Margary by the hips back to him.

Kissing even harder now, Margary undid the belt around his tunic. Once tossed aside, she began lifting the tunic over his head. His mail shirt was next, and not knowing how to remove it, Margary reached back up to his face instead. But he turned his back toward her, indicating that she needed to unclasp the shirt down his back. With the last clasp released, Edric shed the mail shirt with what sounded like loud rainfall. He then pulled his shoulders back to stretch them unrestrained by the shirt. She could see even beneath his wool undershirt that he was incredibly strong. She could also smell how desperately he needed a bath. When he turned back to face her, she smiled.

"I believe that is the first smile I have seen on your face in ten years," he said softly, cupping her cheek.

"I believe you need to wash," she said coyly back to him.

He laughed—the first laugh she had heard from him in ten years. Then he leaned down to kiss her once more and said, "I can only imagine how rancid I must smell to you."

He then put his arms over his head and tugged his shirt off his body. Feeling suddenly timid and nervous, Margary turned away from him as though to give him privacy. But he pulled her back around and said in her ear, "Stay with me, Margary." And weakening at the knees for what felt like the tenth time that night, she did.

Slowly, she found her hands on his waist. As she trailed her fingers just along the inside of his waistline, he took in a sharp breath. Then, as if to help her, he lowered his pants until they fell to the floor around his ankles. Margary stared at his eyes but yearned to look at the rest of him. Stepping away from her, Edric walked towards the tub, giving her a quick glance at his manhood. Her breath caught in her throat. He looked familiar and unfamiliar at the same time.

Examining his back as he stepped over the edge, she noted how defined his muscles had become and how broad his chest was. She then saw a thick purple scar across his lower back. Walking closer to him to get a better look, she also saw a much lighter scar on his side. And then, to her dismay, yet another long scar just above his elbow.

He lowered himself into the water carefully, sighing as he did so. Once in, he put his head completely under and stayed there for some time. Coming back up, he rubbed the water from his eyes and reached for the bar of soap. But Margary's hand grasped it first.

"May I?" she asked softly.

He turned his head to look into her eyes and smiled a delicious smile—one that she had replayed in her head over and over again during the first years he had been away. It was the boyish smile he always gave her when they were about to make love.

Pulling her sleeves back, she dipped her hands in the water to wet the soap and rubbed it between them. Then she started massaging the soap into his back. Edric's muscles felt so firm under her hands. He leaned his head to both sides as she rubbed his neck muscles, and then she slowly pushed him forward to rub his back. Other than the sound of her hands running across his back and the fire smoldering in the hearth, the room was silent.

Tracing the largest scar on his back, she asked, "What happened here?"

"A French swordsman at the siege of Châlus. I was next to His Majesty as he took the blow from a crossbow that led to his death. I was running toward him after he took the hit and turned my back on an opponent. Thankfully, my armor took the brunt of the hit. It could have been a deadly blow."

Moving her hands along his back, she then asked, "And what of this one?"

"An arrow somewhere in the first few years of being away."

"And here?" she asked, running her fingers over the scar on his arm.

He laughed and said, "Thomas stabbed me with his knife when I pulled him off our senior commander's mistress."

"Why am I not surprised?" Margary mused, running her hands back up to his neck and pulling him back to the edge of the tub where she could scrub his chest. Thomas had been Edric's closest friend when they were youths, and even as a young boy, he was always chasing women, young and old.

"We always laughed about how he would die happily at the hands of an angry husband. But instead, he got sick from a shallow wound." Pausing to recall the memory, he then concluded, "We buried him at sea off the coast of France." Wrapping her arms around his neck, Margary placed her cheek against his ear.

"You have lived through many horrors. It is a wonder you are still...you."

"The promise of you saved me." Turning his head toward her cheek, he kissed her softly. She then met his lips, and Edric gently nibbled her lip. She wrapped her arms back around his chest and felt the water start to seep into her dress sleeves. But she didn't care, for the feel of his skin against her fingertips was waking up every fiber of her being that she thought had died in the last decade.

As her fingers trailed down his chest onto his abdomen, Edric took in a sharp breath, and then, still keeping his lips on hers, he turned in the tub to face her. Grabbing her face between both wet hands, he rose out of the tub onto his knees to embrace her. Running his hands through her hair, he began to kiss her neck. Margary closed her eyes and savored every shockwave that ran through her body with each brush of his lips. His hands trailed down to her collarbone and chest, where he began unlacing her dress. All the while, he kept his lips on her neck. With her dress loosened, Edric began slipping her sleeves down her shoulders. The dress still clung onto her breasts, not willing to fall away just yet. He pulled his lips away from her neck and stared at her.

"You are more beautiful than I remembered," he whispered.

Margary stepped back so he could see all of her. In the glow of the firelight, she tugged her dress and chemise slowly down over her breasts, letting the clothing fall off her body. Standing naked in front of him with her dress in a pool at her feet, she let Edric see her fully. As close as they once were, she would have never felt the confidence to stand in such a way in front of him, but now she wanted to be seen. She could almost feel Edric's eyes graze over her entire body, taking in her soft, ample breasts, her pale, delicate pink nipples, her alabaster skin, and her red hair falling around her shoulders, tickling the top of her buttocks.

Edric reached his arm out of the water to beckon her toward him. Grasping his hand, she let him help her climb into the small tub. Still on his knees, he buried his face on her belly and down into the thick golden hair between her legs. Breathing her in, he groaned, and she slowly began to sink herself into the water. She knelt down, but Edric gently picked her up and wrapped her legs around his waist. Seated together with the warm water embracing them, Margary felt the firmness of his manhood press between their bellies.

Edric whispered, "Now I have truly come home."

Overcome with emotion yet again, Margary felt tears well up in her eyes and simply nodded as she rested her cheek on his shoulder. They sat entwined for some time, but then the persistence of their desire took over the moment, and they started kissing again, this time with a renewed urgency. Margary felt herself moving up and down his manhood with her belly, and, not getting all that she needed from it, she took him in her hand and let herself learn him again. Edric leaned his head back against the tub and groaned with desire as she kissed his neck and explored him. He had changed, or she had forgotten what it felt like to touch him. But she knew it would take the rest of her life to ever tire of touching the different parts of him.

She could see his pleasure mounting, and he firmly grabbed her wrist to stop her. Looking at her with a passionate glimmer in his eyes, he turned her around so her back was against his chest and cupped her breasts in his hands. Leaving one hand on her breast, he trailed the other one between her legs and held her. She couldn't take the pressure building up in her and started to slowly move her hips to rub herself against him.

Edric had never learned how to pleasure her by hand—in truth, they hadn't had time to master their passion before he left. But in his absence, she had learned how to make herself reach oblivion. And so, grabbing his fingers, she put them on the softest part of her womanhood and showed him how to touch her. Eyes closed with her head on his chest, she slowly let his fingers go so he could proceed on his own. She felt her breath begin to quicken and started moving her body between his firm thighs. Taking his other hand off of her breast, he moved it down to her as well and danced his fingers around her entrance.

It was such an exquisite feeling, yet something burned deep within her, and she rose out of his embrace and turned to face him. Instead of staying in the water, Edric stood up quickly and stepped out of the tub. He laid the towels on a fur rug in front of the hearth. Taking an extra towel, he helped her out of the tub and wrapped her in it. Then, picking her up in both arms, he carried her to the rug and laid her down gently.

Pulling the towel away from her, he laid his wet body on top of hers and began to kiss her again. Margary could not wait another moment and grasped his manhood to pull him to her. As he slowly lowered himself into her, they both gasped with the surprise and shock of pleasure. He wanted to start moving himself back and forth, but Margary held his hips firmly so she could adjust to him.

"Now I am also home," she whispered in his ear.

Edric pulled his head back to look into her eyes and saw the desire and firelight dancing in them. She couldn't keep him from moving a moment longer, and once he started pushing in and out of her, neither of them could last. Only moments later, they both found their release around one another, their moans echoing throughout their bedchamber. Edric rolled them over so that he was on his back with Margary on top of him, and the two lay as one while their heartbeats began to slow. With the fire warming their bodies and a wool blanket thrown over her back, they both drifted into sleep.

Waking sometime later, they found the fire had subsided substantially, and the room had darkened. Margary slowly lifted herself off Edric, and grasping his hand, she pulled him into their bed. Burying themselves beneath the bedclothes and entangling around one another, they began to make love again. But this time, it was with much less urgency, as they took their time experiencing the pleasure found in one another.

...

Waking to beams of light cast onto their bed, Margary found Edric's arms wrapped tightly around her. She lay there, listening to his soft breathing in her hair. In a way, every moment of heartache over the last ten years had somehow healed overnight.

Reaching toward the end of one of their blankets without waking him, Margary started tearing at the piece of thread she had been tugging at the evening before. Finally pulling it free, she began to braid the strands together. Tying it into a circle, she placed it over her finger. In her determination, she had not realized that Edric had woken. He reached around her body and grasped her hand. His fingertips brushed the thread on her finger. Stiffening, he pulled himself off of her and left the bed. Confused, Margary sat up and watched his naked figure walk across the bedroom. He bent down to place logs into the hearth and started the fire again. Then, brushing his hands off, he walked toward his clothes and bent down in search of something.

Had she done something wrong? Pulling the large blanket to cover her breasts, she was about to ask Edric what was wrong. But he walked back to Margary. Instead of getting back into the bed, he knelt on the floor next to her side of the bed and grasped her hand with the makeshift ring.

Looking deep into her eyes, the sun shining onto his beautiful, thick brown hair, he pulled off her ring and slipped a gold band down her finger. Margary stared at it as it glistened in the sunlight. It had an intricate botanical engraving on it. She had never seen anything like it.

"I bartered my knife for it before we left the Holy Land, with every hope that you would marry me again."

Moving the ring so she could see every little detail, she found herself overcome by his love for her all these years. Pulling him off his knees to kiss him, she whispered,

"I will marry you every day for the rest of time, Edric."

3

Cecily's Story

The year is 1486.

King Henry VII and Elizabeth of York have just married, uniting the warring houses of Lancaster and York into a new dynasty of English monarchs.

In setting up her household at court, the new Queen Elizabeth includes Cecily, her childhood friend of unremarkable birth, as one of her ladies-in-waiting. Cecily is entirely devoted to her friend and Queen, but an unexpected love turns her world upside down.

The night of January 18, 1486, was frigid with fog rolling off the Thames and settling into the grounds of Westminster Palace. The day itself had brought drizzling rains that did not cease, casting an aura of dreariness about the city. It was not a day that one would associate with the start of a happy and fruitful marriage and, more importantly, a peaceful England. But that is indeed what the day brought.

In a quiet ceremony at Westminster Abbey led by the elderly Cardinal Bourchier, King Henry VII and Elizabeth of the House of York were married within the final dwelling place of past kings and queens. The candlelit ceremony included only the closest family, companions, and advisors to the royal couple.

With the ceremony behind them, the wedded couple returned to Westminster Palace for their wedding feast. Many courtiers had traveled across the country to witness the glorious day, and no expense was spared to honor this great occasion. Even the people celebrating outside the palace walls benefited from the new monarch's generosity, as household staff distributed the surplus of food and drink.

Music and merriment went well into the evening as freezing rain turned to snow. But, per tradition, the royal couple broke off from their party to partake in the final formality to solidify their union. Several male courtiers hollered and offered bawdy jests as the king and queen exited the hall, but the couple seemed unperturbed.

"Are you nervous?" Cecily asked the new bride while brushing her dense blonde hair, which shimmered in the firelight. Elizabeth was renowned for her beauty—a proper English rose, as some called her.

"I can't say I am thrilled about the prying eyes that will surely evaluate every inch of me and every move I make. But beyond that, no, I am not nervous." Then, as though the weight of what was to come finally set in, she turned around and said, "Promise me you will stay."

Cecily's mouth fell agape. "Stay? For the whole time, you mean?"

"Yes. Well, obviously not the whole time. You will, of course, leave with everyone else when the bishop says it is time. But you will wait just outside the door, won't you?"

Cecily saw a look of pleading in her eyes—a look that she was unaccustomed to seeing in her strong and confident friend and now queen.

"Of course, if you wish me to stay, I will. But—" Cecily broke off, lowering her voice slightly. "I thought you were at ease with what is to come?" Elizabeth had certainly said as much only days before when Cecily had escorted her to meet with the king alone in his privy chamber and asked her friend to remain just outside the door for some time.

Elizabeth looked at Cecily and nodded her head.

"I am at ease. It's just that I don't want to walk back to my bedchamber alone or be escorted by one of the king's grooms-men. We can't trust anyone. Not yet." She turned back around for Cecily to continue brushing her hair. "In truth, I just know I will feel different after all is said and done and I am officially his wife. And I want to be able to tell someone about it. Perhaps that is unusual, but it is true."

"You will always have my ear. And, of course, I will wait for you," Cecily replied, setting down the brush and placing Elizabeth's robes over her shoulders.

The journey to the king's bedchamber was across the palace, as Elizabeth was not yet in the queen's chambers. Those chambers were presently occupied by the king's mother. Adding an extra shawl over her shoulders and helping her into new silk slippers, Cecily dabbed rose oil at the nape of Elizabeth's neck and behind her ears. She then gave her mint leaves to chew and held her hand out for the remains. Elizabeth softly spat them into Cecily's hand, smiling at her.

"You think of everything, CeeCee. You always have," Elizabeth said, grasping Cecily's hands into hers. "All right," she said at last. "Best not to keep them waiting any longer."

The two women could hear the bawdiness of some of the king's men as they neared the apartments. Elizabeth had a determined look on her face, which Cecily admired. Had she been in the queen's position, she surely would be breathless and ghostly pale. As they entered the presence chamber and passed through the privy chamber, the noise ceased, and the small crowd parted to allow Elizabeth and her lady access to the bedchamber. Cecily could hardly breathe in as the overwhelming odor of drink and sweat hit her nostrils.

Without a look back, Elizabeth walked gracefully through the doorway and slowed as her husband turned in her direction. The doors closed behind both of them. Only a few members of the court were admitted into this part of the ceremony. Cecily recognized the bishop from the wedding ceremony, who had now donned more modest robes than he had during the wedding. There was also Margaret Beaufort, the king's mother, and four of the king's closest men. Cecily remained next to the closed doors, but Elizabeth nodded ever so slightly to have her join her. She walked up to the queen, and seeing her hold her arms out, Cecily slowly removed the shawl and dressing robe so she was only in her shift. The king briefly nodded toward the bed, and the couple hastened to slip between the sheets.

Out of respect for his queen, the king didn't want Elizabeth to be exposed longer than absolutely necessary. With the couple tucked in neatly, sitting almost shoulder to shoulder, the bishop began blessing the marital bed. Then, on cue, one of the grooms-men pulled the sheets back from the bottom of the bed, and the couple touched their legs together. The Bishop made his final blessing for a fruitful union and led the exodus from the room, with the king's mother and groomsmen trailing him. Cecily looked back at her queen to see if she needed anything further, but her eyes were locked on her husband's. Seeing that she was no longer needed, she too, left the royal couple.

Once outside the door, she was hit once again by the stench of drunken men laughing and carousing. There had to be at least thirty of them. Cecily tried to remain inconspicuous and found the nearest stool just outside the doors. She had no idea how she would be able to tolerate sitting on this stool amongst this crowd for the entire night. At least music had started after the bishop left, so she had something to occupy herself while she waited. But her post was soon discovered as a large, bawdy man with cheeks rosy from drink ambled toward her with a sloppy grin.

"And what do we have here?" he slurred, his eyes watery and his breath foul. Elizabeth stood up instantly, words escaping her.

"Shouldn't you be in bed, pet?" he said again, getting even closer to her.

Finding her voice, she said, "I am the queen's lady. Please step back."

The man laughed and stepped even closer, forcing her against the wall so she could not avoid him pressing upon her.

"This is no place for a young lady, now," he slurred, his eyes shining brightly.

"I am to wait here for Her Majesty," Cecily replied, her voice quieter than she would have liked.

He laughed again. "Then you will be here all night while the king devours her. Surely you would like some company," he said, attempting to be coy.

"I would prefer to be alone, thank you," she retorted.

"In a room full of men with appetites even greater than mine, it would be best not to be found alone," he slurred.

Cecily surveyed the room and then replied sharply, "It seems you are the only person in this room who is being a problem to me."

The man laughed heartily, drawing some glances in their direction. But Elizabeth noticed most men turned back to their own conversations, and many were now pouring over a packed table of cards. Animals, she thought to herself. The man leaned his towering body over hers, placing his hand on the wall above her head. Cecily didn't miss the fact that he practically had to use the wall to steady himself over her.

"Get off," she said fiercely. He looked at her bleary-eyed and smiling.

"No, I quite like the view I have here," he said, leaning his face into her neck.

"Last chance," Cecily said, holding her ground. "Leave me alone or else." His nose brushed her skin.

The man threw his head back and laughed harder than before, and she took that opportunity to pummel her fist into his stomach. He doubled over, letting out a loud groan. His expression was a mix of shock and anger.

"Damn you, girl!" he roared, stumbling against the wall.

Cecily looked at him in horror. *What have I done?* But to her relief, the men in the crowd turned their attention in her direction and had a good laugh at the man's state as he slunk down onto the floor. Several of them came over to haul him to his feet, shoving another ale in his fist and guiding him to a chair.

Completely irritated and shaken, she looked down at her hand, trying to discern how badly she had injured herself. Stretching her fingers, she was grateful that the man was soft around the middle. Had he been firm, she knew her hand would be in much worse shape.

"You need help with your hand," said a voice in her left ear. Cecily started, not having heard anyone come up to her. She looked up and saw a man with genuine concern in his eyes. He had curly black hair and deep honey-brown eyes. His face was tanned—darker than most in the court, and he was significantly taller than the other men in the room. His eyes were so bright and piercing. It was unnerving.

"I am fine, thank you," Cecily replied, finally finding the words.

"Let me see," he said, holding out his large hand for hers.

"No, really, I am perfectly fine," she insisted, but he continued to hold out his hand and gazed at her intently. Giving in, she stuck out her fist for him to examine. He turned over her delicate pale hand in his and pushed ever so slightly on her knuckles. She winced as he did so.

"If you don't treat these, they will become swollen and tender and impossible to use for several days."

"It was hardly that great of a hit," she replied, studying his face. But he looked sideways at her and nodded toward the man she had punched. He was still doubled over, many of his friends laughing around him at his expense.

"I think you underestimate the blow you delivered to Alban. He is particularly drunk tonight, but he is usually made of tougher stuff than that. Come with me. I will fix you up."

"I am fine, thank you," she said again, firmly.

The man sighed and replied, "Believe me, mistress, I know a thing or two about healing after a fight. If you do not treat it soon, you will be hard-pressed to use that hand for weeks." And, as if to solidify his position, he nodded toward the door and said, "Your queen will not be leaving these doors for several hours, if not until morning. You have time to get yourself fixed up."

Cecily looked at the door and back at him. His eyes had gold flecks in them. Cecily found it hard to hold his gaze, as she could almost feel herself being pulled into its black depths. Forcing her focus back onto solid ground, she replied, "Lead the way, then." She nodded toward the door on the opposite wall. Several men turned in their direction as they slipped through the throng of revelers.

"Oy, Thomas!" one of the men around the man named Alban shouted. "Where are you making off to?"

When he did not reply and kept walking, another man with a strong Scottish accent yelled over the crowd, "Try not to be too rough with him, lass! He's still a wee babe!"

In response, the man leading her through the crowd threw up an obscene gesture and continued to lead Cecily out of the bursting, raucous room.

She walked next to the man named Thomas, who did not say anything as they wound their way through the palace and up several flights of steps. Finally, they treaded down a long passageway, and he held a small door open and indicated that she should start climbing up a narrow set of steps. There was hardly any light in the small tower.

"Where are we going?" she asked before entering the stairwell.

"To fix your hand," he replied smoothly.

Cecily wanted to protest, but she also didn't want to seem timid in front of him. Walking through the stairwell, she began trudging up the steps, trusting that each foot would use its intuition to find the next step in the dark. Finally, she reached a small landing with a heavy wooden door. Cecily pressed her back against the stone wall as Thomas slid his body next to hers and expertly unlatched several locks on the door. She swallowed hard, her mouth becoming dry. Was it a mistake to trust and follow this man here? Why would he be leading her to the far end of the palace, through a door that few had access to and one that required multiple keys to unlock?

Cold air rushed into the stairwell as he pushed open the door, causing Cecily to draw in a sharp breath. The man stepped down first and gently grabbed her elbow to help her down. When her feet hit the solid stone ground, she looked around and saw they were standing on the barracks surrounding the entire palace. The snow was still falling, and in some areas, it was as high as her ankles. She peered through one of the many narrow overlooks and felt instantly dizzy from the swirling snow and the height of where they were standing.

"Is this where you push me to my death?" she asked, turning back to where he had stood.

But he had walked over to a large pile of snow and packed it into a hard lump. He smirked at her comment as he made his way back toward her. Reaching for her injured hand, he placed her sore fingers on his palm and rolled the snow over her aching joints.

"The cold will help with the swelling," he said quietly. The two stood in silence, listening as the snowflakes fell softly around them.

Cecily had never been up so high in her life. What it must be like to have this vantage point over the city during the day. Feeling the need to fill the space, she said, "Do you come up here often?"

"No," he replied. "But it is my job to know every passageway leading up to the battlements."

"You are a soldier, then," she said.

"Yes."

"But you must be more than just a soldier to be so close to the king?" she inquired.

"You say it like being *just* a soldier is not enough," he replied, a little cooly.

"Not at all, it's just...most people close to any king are generally of noble birth."

"And that would impress you?" he replied steadily.

"No!" Cecily said awkwardly. "I suppose I am just making conversation."

"Well, I am a soldier. That is who I am and what I have always been." He seemed distant.

"Okay," Cecily said quietly. The two stood in awkward silence for some time as Thomas placed new snow over her fingers. Her hand was now so numb she couldn't tell if the trauma from the blow or the cold was actually causing more pain.

"And what of you?" he asked.

"I am not a soldier," she replied.

"I wouldn't be so sure of that," he said, grinning as he turned her hand over in his.

"I have been with the queen since we were girls. We became friends around the time she was engaged to the Dauphin of France. My father was a soldier for the Yorkists and died when I was a baby. My mother was part of the queen's household. She died of the sweat when little Edward lost the throne to that usurper." Her mind was filled with the painful memories of that period of her life. "When her brothers were taken to the tower, the queen's mother swept all of us away into exile to keep us alive. I owe them everything."

"So you have lived your life only at court."

"Mostly," she replied. "But when we were in exile, we lived in the countryside away from everyone. It's the happiest part of my life, even though it was shadowed by sheer terror."

Cecily didn't know why she was being so open with him. Perhaps it was because no one had ever bothered to ask her anything about herself. When he didn't say anything aside from a nod, she asked,

"Where did you spend your childhood?"

"In trees," he replied.

Cecily looked hard at him and saw his eyes smiling.

"I grew up in the Midlands. The area is known for its dense forests. Legend holds that Robin Hood might have lived there. I always pretended I was him."

"Did you have playmates?"

"My brothers." His eyes now seemed distant, and the two stood in silence again. Cecily felt a chill run down her spine. She had been so on edge about being alone with this man she did not know, in a part of the palace she certainly should not be in, that she had not realized how cold she had become.

"Your hand will not be as tender in the morning now. We should go back," he said. Cecily nodded and tossed the snow over the edge of the wall.

Looking one last time at the abyss below, he said, "You should see it during the day."

"I would like that," she replied.

Following him back down the stairwell and through the palace corridors, the two made their way to the king's chambers. But before heading back into the antechamber, Thomas veered them through another chamber and into what felt like a large storage closet. A small wooden door was opposite them.

"Through here is another entrance to the king's bedchamber. Only a few know about this entrance. This is where your queen will come out in the morning. You can wait for her here. You shouldn't be bothered by any of my friends here."

Cecily swallowed hard and looked around. Among some random wooden furnishings, there was a chair and a small table. He indicated that she should sit there to wait. Doing as he bid, she wrapped her arms around herself. She was cold and tired, and her hand ached from the ice.

"Here," Thomas said, pulling off his cloak. "You must be freezing." He wrapped it around her arms. "I will be back in a few hours to collect the sheets. You don't need to worry about that."

"What?" Cecily asked, perplexed.

"I am in charge of taking the sheets to Cardinal Bouchier—to adhere to the formality of this whole thing."

"I don't understand." Thomas looked at her, somewhat bemused.

"I will let your mistress explain." And then, with a slight bow, he left Cecily. In the darkness of the small room, lit only by a small torch, her mind raced about what had just happened. He had been kind yet distant. He went out of his way to help her with her hand yet didn't bother asking her name. She replayed their conversation and the different facial expressions he had.

And those eyes—the way they practically stripped off her skin and peered into her soul. She fell asleep in the chair, wrapped in his cloak, dreaming of those eyes.

...

"Cecily!"

She started, her head slipping off her hand. The stone surrounding the only small window in the room framed a picture of the pale pink and blue sunrise. The queen had her hand on her elbow to rouse her awake. Her mistress was dressed in her nightclothes and the fur shawl she had placed over her shoulders hours before. Cecily stood quickly and gathered up the cloak.

"I see you found your way to the king's private entrance. I forgot to tell you to wait here in all the confusion of yesterday."

Cecily nodded, saying, "One of his men told me this was where I should meet you."

"I can see that," she replied, nodding with a slight smile to the cloak. "You met Thomas, I presume." Cecily nodded. "Well, you can leave his cloak here—I am sure he will grab it later." But Cecily hung onto it.

"I'd like to return it to him—to thank him." The queen looked bemused.

"I am sure you would," she said slyly, a smile creeping across her face as she turned to leave the storage room.

"Don't we need to gather up the sheets?" Cecily asked.

Elizabeth chuckled and said, "Thomas already grabbed them. That's when he told me you were still here waiting for me." And, as an afterthought, she added, "Everyone is very anxious to prove my innocence and verify our consummation."

"I don't understand," Cecily said.

"And I love you for it," Elizabeth replied, smiling. "I will explain it when we get back to my chambers."

The queen was good to her word and described her night in what felt like too much detail to Cecily. As she brushed through her mistress's hair, Cecily felt the blood rouging her cheeks in surprise at what had transpired between her and the king. But she also felt somewhat sorry for Elizabeth and said as much.

"I am sorry it had to be so public your first time. It must not have been easy to know that your linens would be inspected by a man of the church."

Elizabeth looked up at her, somewhat mischievously. "If it had been our first time, I might have welcomed that sympathetic look on your face. But we took it into our own hands to do it on our own terms." Cecily looked at her, perplexed. Then she recalled the undisturbed hour she had waited outside for Elizabeth and her betrothed before they were married.

"But what of the sheets?" Cecily said, shocked.

"Oh, Henry took care of it."

And when Cecily saw the king later for mass, she noted a thin piece of white cloth wrapped around a finger on his left hand. Cecily suspected that he had drawn his own blood to spare his wife the embarrassment of tradition.

Following mass, Cecily looked for Thomas, hoping to return the cloak. But he was nowhere to be found. Later that night, during yet another celebratory feast, Cecily also scanned the room for him, but to no avail. The queen caught her gaze at one point, raising her eyebrows in her direction.

"No luck finding your savior from last night?" Elizabeth jested that evening as Cecily helped to ready her for bed. Cecily frowned at her mistress. "I heard about your little incident last night—something about throwing your fist into one of the king's soldiers' bellies. I will gain quite the reputation if my ladies are known as fighters."

"I didn't mean to cause attention. I was being harassed."

"Oh, I heard all about it. No, you have every right to attack anyone who would force themselves upon you. I have heard

Alban often gets sloppy when he drinks to excess but is otherwise reliable."

The two women sat in silence as Cecily once again rubbed rose oil into her mistress's neck and offered her mint leaves to chew.

"I know I do not have to say this to you, but following strange men you do not know may not be your best play here at court, for your sake and mine. People cannot be trusted, and you should know that those who try to get close to you are likely trying to gather information about me that may be used against me and the king."

"And you think Thomas is untrustworthy?" Cecily asked.

Elizabeth seemed to think hard as she chewed the leaves and then, spitting them out, said, "As your queen, I can assure you that Thomas has our best interests. But as your friend, I cannot speak to his motives."

Cecily felt somewhat chided at what Elizabeth had said. Of course, she knew all of this, but she also didn't want to admit that being used never even crossed her mind the moment she locked eyes with Thomas. He was different—not that she had any other man to compare him to—but she knew in her bones that he was good.

As the two women walked the torch-lit corridors with guards

stationed throughout, Cecily felt apprehensive about returning to the room where she would await her mistress. Elizabeth had promised she wouldn't stay all night, which was just as well because Cecily had no sleep the previous night. But she also felt a nagging tug that maybe the longer she stayed, the more likely she would run into Thomas.

To her disappointment, he never showed up, nor did he the night after. Had it not been for the cloak slung over the back of her wooden chair in her small bedchamber, Cecily would have begun wondering if being on the battlements with him was just a dream.

...

The court was scheduled to move on to Greenwich a week after the wedding. Cecily had overheard the king telling his wife how he wished to expand the existing palace into something much larger and grander. He wanted to spend more time there to formulate his vision. Cecily looked forward to leaving London to explore a new royal residence away from the city but also couldn't help wondering if "her savior," as Elizabeth kept referring to him, would ever surface again.

On the final day before the court was to depart Westminster, Cecily found herself strolling along a corridor, watching how the small rectangles of light spilled onto the stones, the dust particles dancing as they floated softly toward the ground. Footsteps walking quickly from behind her made her move to one side of the corridor, but she kept her eyes downcast at the light beams. The figure walked past her and then stopped abruptly.

"You."

Cecily looked up and saw those golden eyes looking at her. So he was real then.

"You," she replied back. A slight smile broke out across his face. He didn't speak right away as he held her gaze, his fingers thumbing the sword next to his hip.

"What were you looking at?" he asked, shifting his eyes to the ground where she had been focusing.

"Nothing."

"Nothing?" he prodded.

Cecily shifted between her feet and then said hesitantly, "I was looking at how the light danced down the corridor."

Thomas stared at her a moment longer, then came up next to her and turned to face the same direction down the hall. They stood together in silence, watching the rainbow of colors.

"Not many people would notice the subtleties of how the light reflects through these windows."

She felt her nerves starting to take over her body and mind as he looked at her. To fill the silent void, she said, "You have been away. I tried to return your cloak."

"Yes, I was in need of that, actually," he said, smirking. "I left early the morning after the wedding with a delegate of the king's men to ensure the nobles in the old Lancastrian forces were well aware that the marriage was solidified. I only just returned."

"Is there still a question of who should be on the throne?" she asked.

Thomas shifted his feet. "There will always be those that question any monarch's claim, but I think all of England is unified in being grateful civil war is behind us."

"What a relief," Cecily said with an edge of bitterness.

"Are you looking forward to going to Greenwich tomorrow?" Thomas asked, changing the subject.

"Yes, I believe so. I hear it is beautiful, and the city has become somewhat stifling. I miss the country air and the scenery."

"I prefer the country as well, but there is beauty in the city, too," he said.

"I have yet to see it," she replied somewhat bitterly. She had grown tired of being restricted to the palace walls and unable to go outside, even though it had been cold and dreary since they had arrived in London.

"Then let me show you," he said, his eyes flashing.

Elizabeth looked at him, surprised. He turned back down the corridor they had both been walking and beckoned her with a nod to come with him. As she followed, she could hear her queen's words in the back of her head. *Following men you do not know may not be your best play here at court.*

Within a few minutes of weaving through the palace, Cecily understood where he was taking her. He opened the familiar door, and the two trudged up the long, spiral suitcase in the tower to the battlements where they had been the night of the wedding. Thomas unlocked the various latches again, and with a shove of his shoulder, the door sprung open, spilling them onto its narrow walkway. Instead of dizzying snowfall, Cecily's eyes were met by an endless expanse of buildings.

From her vantage point, she could see the Thames flowing ever so steadily. And there was the White Tower in the distance, where her mistress' brothers had disappeared. No trees were in sight, undoubtedly burned for firewood and city construction. She walked around the battlements as far as she could, Thomas trailing silently behind her. She stopped when she had a view of the impressive Abbey where the king and queen had been married.

"How remarkable that human hands built all of this," she said in awe.

Thomas stepped next to her and said, after a pause, "What confounds me is that our hands can simultaneously create so beautifully and destroy so viciously."

Cecily turned to look up at him. "I imagine you have seen much of both, given your occupation," she replied.

Thomas subtly nodded his head, his gaze becoming distant. Cecily resisted her urge to reach out and grab his hand. He was a hardened soldier who had been on the battlefield only months, if not weeks, before this moment. And yet, something in those eyes showed an undeniable gentleness.

"Thank you for taking me up here," Cecily said, folding her hands into one another to keep from reaching out to him.

"I may get a severe scolding if we are found out," he said with a crooked smile. "But I hoped I would run into you when I returned so I could show you." Cecily smiled and started heading back for the door.

"Let's not risk a scolding, then," she said, grinning at him over her shoulder.

Thomas remained in place for a moment longer and then started to follow her. The walk back was quiet between them until they returned down the corridor where they had initially met.

"How can I get you your cloak?" Cecily asked as they stopped back at where the light had once danced onto the floor. It had now shifted with the hour and was no longer as captivating.

"Keep it for now," Thomas replied. "It will give me an excuse to meet you again in Greenwich."

Cecily's heart jumped. He turned to walk away, a slight smile playing across his face.

"You don't even know my name," she called out, confused by his words.

He turned back to her, and smiling, he said, "I don't need to know your name to know I want to see you again."

Heart pounding in her chest even more, Cecily stood rooted to her spot, watching him turn into what were the king's chambers. She had certainly delighted in hearing he wanted to see her again. Yet, he didn't exactly reassure her of his intentions either. Had Elizabeth been correct? Or was all of this so foreign to her that she didn't understand the rules of the game?

...

The palace at Greenwich was sprawling and cold during early

February. Courtiers were still finding their place in the new regime, and many tried to worm their way into the queen's favor by forcing daughters and nieces into her household. Elizabeth told Cecily how two-faced many of them were, as some families had turned their backs on her mother, the former queen, only to now come crawling back to her to offer their unwavering loyalty.

"You can trust no one here," Elizabeth said repeatedly to Cecily. Of course, the queen knew this all too well with all of the atrocities committed against her family for access to the crown.

Despite her increasingly busy role as one of the queen's closest ladies, Cecily was grateful that Greenwich offered her more opportunity for sleep. The queen's bedchamber was attached by a private corridor to the king's, so Cecily no longer had to wait for the queen to return from her husband's bed. Often, he spent the night with her in her own chambers, so Cecily was forced out of her duties to the queen early in the night. Thus, she was able to spend the evenings as she chose. For her, that usually meant in the company of a book, as she had little interest in court gossip that the rest of the ladies would chirp to one another in the queen's absence.

The only other way she could envision spending her idle evenings was in Thomas' company. She had seen him a handful of times since they had been at Greenwich, but they had always been surrounded by others. They had only exchanged quick smiles at one another, never passing a word between them.

Sometimes, Thomas gave her a hard stare that sent shockwaves through her body.

Cecily tried to convince herself that she likely wouldn't be as concerned with him if she had more to occupy her mind. But then, when she'd see him next, her heart would flip in her chest, and her breath would quicken. Why did he have such an effect on her? It was maddening. And she still had his cloak, which had become a burden to her at this point because not only did it no longer smell of him, but it appeared he had no desire to ask for it back.

"Have you returned that silly cloak yet?" Elizabeth asked her coyly one afternoon while she was bathing.

"No," Cecily grumbled. She tried not to sound affected by the question, but her friend knew her too well.

"If you want to get rid of it, just find a way to get it back to him. He's always in Henry's privy chamber before I go to his bed. You can accompany me tonight, give it to him yourself, and then be done with it. I can see it's eating away at you."

"It is not!" Cecily said in defiance. "Besides, you likely won't go to your husband's bed tonight anyway. I had the laundress bring up rags for you earlier this week. My courses just finished, so yours should have already started. I would imagine you will want to keep to yourself until they have passed."

Elizabeth said nothing, the water stilling in the tub. Cecily was busy combing through her hair when her head finally jerked up, a realization hitting her. "Unless..." she said, putting down the comb and walking toward the other side of the tub to look at her friend. A small smile pulled across Elizabeth's cheeks, and she nodded in response to Cecily's shocked expression.

"I think I am with child."

"Oh, Lizzy, that's wonderful!" Cecily said, calling her friend her childhood name. "Are you certain?"

"How should I know?" she said, smiling bigger now as she sat up in the tub to hug her knees. "My breasts are tender. Every time Henry grabs them, I want to scream out. And my nipples look different, don't they?" she said, rising out of the tub. Cecily blushed at the intimate details shared with her about the king. But, scanning her friend's chest, she did notice something was just a hint different about her.

"When will you tell him?"

"I don't know. I only realized it last night when the aching in my legs was nonexistent, and my other usual signs of bleeding were nowhere to be felt." Silence hung between them as they both processed this information.

"You're going to be a mother, Lizzy," Cecily said tenderly.

"I am going to give birth to a king," Elizabeth said. She seemed distant, her thoughts clearly wrapped up in the future.

...

Cecily did accompany Elizabeth to Henry's room that night in search of Thomas. Elizabeth pointed out that, remarkably, Cecily had forgotten the cloak she had been so eager to return. Cecily ignored the comment, hiding a slight smile from her friend.

The pair entered through the privy chamber rather than the private entrance to the king's bed. A few men were seated at a small table with the king, a game of cards between them. A quick scan of the heads told Cecily he was not among the group. She tried to keep the disappointment from showing on her face and body.

The queen slid over to the king, giving him a soft kiss on the cheek. She then took a seat that had been vacated by one of the men so she could join in the game. Cecily hung back, observing.

"No Thomas tonight, then?" Elizabeth asked casually, holding up her cards.

"I suspect he is halfway to France already," the king replied nonchalantly.

"Why France?" the queen asked, shooting a look toward Cecily over her hand of cards.

"I am sending him as an emissary. There is trouble in Brittany, and I don't want to see it fall to the French." Cecily knew that the king would do whatever he could to keep his land there, as it had been his place of exile for over a decade before the Battle of Bosworth Field.

"When did you assign him the task?" the queen replied casually.

"This afternoon."

"You know how Thomas is, Your Majesty," one of the men at the table broke in. "He will never wait around when something has to be done. I suspect he is probably already gone." Cecily had been walking around the table to be behind her queen and asked to be dismissed. Elizabeth nodded, looked at her carefully, and bid her goodnight.

Cecily couldn't help it, but she felt devastated at the thought that he was no longer at court. Furthermore, he had yet to seek her out at any point during their stay at Greenwich thus far, even though he had told her he wanted to see her again. Was he stringing her along, or worse, setting her up to use her for information against the queen as she had been warned?

As she walked back to her room, she felt disgusted with

herself. She had never so much as thought about a man and had never allowed anyone to enter her mind the way he had. She had lost control of herself. And she hated him for it. Yet, she knew that to give him that much credit when they had barely known each other was unfair to him. And childish of her. That's how she really felt. She felt like a child.

Her emotions were raging through her veins as she turned the corner to the corridor of her room. Without slowing down to round the corner, she ran right into none other than the man she was furious with.

"You!" she said, angrier than she would have liked. She had forgotten how devastated she had been only moments before when she learned that he was likely already on his way to France.

"Something wrong?" he asked far too casually, drawing back from her after she had steadied herself on her feet. She had run right into his hard chest. Cecily caught her breath and found her voice.

"You were rumored to be halfway to France already."

"So I planned to be." He smiled at her, making her feel more infuriated.

"Well, why aren't you?" she pressed him with irritation. His golden eyes burrowing into her nearly threw her off balance again. While she was furious with him, she couldn't help but notice the confused expression on his face.

"I seem to have left an article of clothing in your care," he said tentatively. Cecily didn't say anything, a blank expression overtaking her face. "My cloak. You have my cloak," he said, still looking at her with a confused expression.

Cecily gaped at him. "And that's why you haven't left for France yet—because you need your cloak," she said with an edge in her voice.

"Yes," he said matter-of-factly.

Cecily felt the disappointment once again start to rise up in her body, but she squelched it by walking around him and down the corridor into her chamber. Opening the door and taking a few deep breaths while holding onto the chair the cloak had been draped over, she closed her eyes and willed her resolve to come back to her. Cecily turned to leave her room, but he was standing in the doorway. A fire had been lit earlier in the evening, and she could see its glow dancing in his eyes. She walked to him and placed the cloak in his hands.

"Thank you for your kindness that night in Westminster," she said quietly, finally gaining control of herself. He nodded, and then, with nothing more to say, she reached for the door as though to close it, but he didn't move.

"I am sorry I did not keep my promise to see you again before I had to leave."

"Why didn't you?" Cecily blurted out before she could let the apology settle between them.

He thought for a moment and then replied, "The logical answer, and the biggest truth, is that I have been busy on the king's orders. It seems there are only a few of us he trusts, and since I was with him in Brittany and fought next to him in battle, I have been delegated some important tasks which need my undivided attention."

"And the lesser truth?" Cecily asked.

"I couldn't get caught up with a distraction." And, with his eyes piercing hers, he said more softly, "You are a distraction to me, Cecily.

There, he had said her name. Finally, she thought, breathing a sigh of relief. She had felt so inconsequential to him that he had not even bothered with her name. And yet, some part of her knew that she had made an impression on him. Why would he have put that much effort into helping her with her hand that night of the wedding when he could have been celebrating with his friends?

"Why be so nice to me that night, then?" she replied, speaking her thoughts before she could stop them. His eyes were ablaze, a soft black curl of hair falling next to his brow.

"Because I could not stay away from you that night. I have been drawn to you since the moment I first saw you." Cecily felt the air catch in her throat, her heart beginning to pound in her ears. Every sense was heightened as he drew slightly closer to her, just one step.

"And when did you first see me?" she whispered, looking up at him.

"At the wedding. You were so focused on your tasks for the queen and so curious about the Abbey that you did not even see me. And I know because my eyes never left your face." He dropped his head as if in an apology.

"Since then, you have acted like you do not care for me—like you do not even know I exist."

"I suppose I have given you no reason to think otherwise," he said. Cecily nodded. "But that is far from the truth. The fact that I forgot to ask you your name is evidence enough that I had already learned who you were."

Cecily's mouth had gone dry. She couldn't believe she was hearing him correctly. She had yearned for him since that night, and her desire to see him again made her feel like she was spiraling out of control.

And she had something else burning within her. Lust, she thought to herself. She wanted him. Some part of her was trying to pull him into her, wanting him to become a part of her. This is what she had always been warned about growing up. To avoid these feelings—these temptations. Cecily backed away a step.

"You do not feel the same," Thomas said matter-of-factly. Cecily shook her head, but it wasn't to tell him she didn't feel that way. It was to shake away the yearning for him coursing through her veins.

"Perhaps I misread you. My apologies if I offended you," Thomas said quietly, turning to leave through the doorway.

"Wait," Cecily said, grabbing for his hand. He turned slowly back toward her. Still holding his hand, she couldn't find the words, but she knew she couldn't let him go either. So she pulled him closer to her—her heart pounding against her chest. "You did not misread me. I just don't know what you want from me." And, his eyes still burning into her, she added, "I just don't know how to be in this situation."

"And what situation is that?" he asked, a slight smile creeping across his lips.

"Whatever this...is," she said hesitantly, using her free hand to indicate the remaining space between them.

"Try to explain it to me," he urged, his breath ragged. Cecily searched his face, trying to find the words to explain everything she had been thinking and feeling since first meeting him.

"I have been told how to act, feel, and think in front of men all my life. And I have been warned it is a sin to have the feelings I have felt since that night on the battlements." And, suddenly realizing what anyone would say to Thomas being almost in her bedchamber, she added, "You should not be here."

But he didn't move. Instead, he looked hard at her and said, "Do you want me to leave?"

It took Cecily only a moment to shake her head. Of course she didn't want him to leave. She wanted him to pull her into him, to know what it was like to be wrapped in his strong arms.

"Don't let anyone else tell you how you should feel, Cecily."

Feeling as though she had waited for permission to disregard everyone else but herself, she stepped toward him and placed her hand on his chest. He put his hand over hers and pulled her closer into an embrace—the embrace she had dreamt about those past few weeks. They stood rooted to the ground, wrapped in each other's arms, him swaying her softly in the glow of the torches lining the corridor behind them and the fire burning from within.

He tilted her chin up with his warm, rough fingertips and

looked into her eyes. Slowly, he leaned down and brushed the softest whisper of a kiss against her rose-colored lips. He pulled back to look at her. She licked her lips in anticipation of more. Recognizing her desire for more, he leaned down and kissed her again. Cecily felt her legs give slightly, and sensing her weakening, Thomas pulled her into his chest.

Their lips pressed harder together, moving with their breath as though they were in a dance. Thomas placed both his hands on her back—the span of his palms to fingertips covering most of her. She put her hands on his hips, pulling him closer to her. As their kisses intensified, Cecily felt a fire burn between them. She wanted his hands to roam beyond her back. She could feel her desire for more of him pumping throughout her body, as though all the blood coursing through her veins settled right between her hips. A yearning such as this had never taken hold of her body. She felt him harden between them, his manhood pressing into her pelvis, and she tried not to show her shock.

Without thinking of anything but her desire, Cecily grabbed his hand and gently tugged him out of the doorway and into her room. He closed the door softly behind her, causing her heart rate to increase even more than it already was at the thought of someone finding them. Before she could give it a second thought, she was back in his arms as he pressed her against the wall where the door had just been. His hands broke free of their place on her back and began roaming over her shoulders and arms. Then, to her shock and delight, he trailed his fingers across her bodice and pulled her sleeve down, slowly exposing her breast.

Cecily was dizzy with pleasure. She might have told him to stop if she had her wits about her because she was afraid to show that part of herself. But something else entirely had taken over her body and mind. She found herself wanting to be seen, wanting to be touched. He reached his hand down into her bodice to free the soft mound, and he instantly placed his lips around her rose-pink nipple. She sucked in a rush of air with delight as his warm, wet mouth took hold of her. His tongue encircled her, tantalizing her. Pulling off of her with a firm suck that was shockingly pleasurable, he slipped her other sleeve down. He offered the same treatment to the other nipple while firmly holding the first one in his hand.

Cecily didn't know what to do with her body. She wanted to crawl out of her clothes, to free herself, and to feel him unrestricted by the material. And mostly, she wanted his hands and, dare she imagine it, his mouth lower. As though trying to shake her desires from her mind, she pulled Thomas back up to her and put her mouth firmly against his again. He pressed her into the wall, much harder this time, to where she almost cried out in pain from his manhood pushing into her pelvis through their clothes. He withdrew softly as though sensing he was being too rough. He reached up and caressed her face, looking into her eyes, his arm pressed against her bare breast. With his other hand, he stroked her hair, which reached the top of her waist.

"I should not go further with you, Cecily, as much as it splits me in half to say." And then, more quietly, he added, "I will not ruin you."

Cecily looked at him with fire in her eyes. "Who has told you I would be ruined?"

"You know you would be—at least to everyone else. I suppose even I have a reputation to uphold," Thomas said breathlessly against her lips, kissing them again.

"Don't let anyone else tell you how you should feel, Thomas." He drew back from her, still holding her head, a small smile breaking across his face.

"Throwing my own advice back at me?" he said, a mischievous smile breaking across his face.

"I would hate for us to miss out on something incredible just because of what others think," Cecily said, surprised at herself as the words flowed out of her mouth. His golden eyes were ablaze with desire.

"That would be a shame," he said with a sultry smile.

And once again, he pressed into her and kissed her. But while his lips strayed no farther than her mouth and neck, his hands began to roam just as she had hoped they would. He gripped her backside and pulled her close. She started rocking her hips into him. A low moan escaped from his mouth as she gasped at the contact between her pelvis and his manhood.

His fingertips began running along the sides of her thighs until they started pulling up her gown. Cecily found herself helping drag the fabric up, and once it was high enough, he snuck his hand under the hem and trailed his fingers along her inner thigh. She gasped, her body yearning for him to inch those fingers higher.

As if reading her mind, Thomas danced his fingers up her thigh and settled at the soft folds between her legs. His thumb trailed her innermost silken skin at the apex of her thighs, causing her to cry out into his shoulder with pleasure. His mouth still on her neck, he whispered in her ear to ask if she wanted him to keep going, but she ground her hips into his hand, which told him all he needed to know.

Once again, he brushed his thumb gently down her delicate skin. Another finger reached further back, sliding across the glossy fluid that had formed around her entrance. Using his wet fingertip, he ran his finger down her over and over again, noticing how the pleasure caused her chest to rise and fall. Keeping his hand in place between her legs, he pulled her away from the wall and placed his back against it, turning her so her back was against his chest. With one hand on her breast, the other between her legs, and his mouth buried in her hair, he continued his mission of rubbing her gently and coaxing her to her pinnacle.

Cecily could feel the pleasure building in her. As he caressed the silken skin between her legs that she had only ever dared to touch herself on the longest of nights, she felt that all the heat and blood in her body was converging right where his hand was. Her legs started to give in as he rubbed, her own hips grinding against his hand to increase the pressure. His movements remained consistent until her body went rigid with climax, and she gasped breathlessly in delight as everything became weightless. Thomas had to bear her weight as she burst all around his fingertips.

Heart still pounding in her ears and between her thighs, she was glad Thomas kept his warm hand between her legs until she began to relax into him. She rolled her head around his chest, savoring the resolution within her. He kissed her head and whispered in her ear,

"Thank you." She smiled with her eyes still closed and said in a low, sultry voice that was utterly foreign to her,

"I am the one who should be thanking you." And then she turned to him, looked down at his straining breeches, and said with a seriousness taking over her expression, "Tell me what to do with you."

Thomas looked at her with such genuine affection in his eyes. But he shook his head, brushing her hair out of her face.

"I would give anything to have your hands around me. But tonight, my pleasure is in seeing your pleasure."

She leaned into him, still savoring the resolution from her climax. He held her against the wall for several moments until footsteps rang down the corridor just next to the one that led to her chambers.

"When do you leave?" Cecily asked, reality settling in more quickly than she'd like. She knew he should leave sooner rather than later so they were not discovered.

"Tomorrow at dawn," he nearly croaked.

"I don't want you to go," Cecily said into his chest. Thomas didn't say anything but kept stroking her hair. Finally, he pulled her back from him and looked down into her eyes. Cecily tried to burn the image of him into her mind.

"I will seek you out the moment I return," Thomas promised her, sealing it with a final kiss on her lips. Then, as if to move while she had the courage to do so, Cecily gathered up the cloak and gave it to him before opening the door to peer down the corridor. He nodded his thanks to her and exited, keeping his footsteps soft as he walked down the hallway. Cecily hoped he would find the silken favor she had tucked into the cloak pocket before he got too far from England.

...

Biting winds and unrelenting rains brought spring to England. In May, the queen's happy news was finally made public, and the court was anticipating the arrival of the first heir of the new Tudor dynasty.

Elizabeth was blooming. Being with child made her all the more radiant. Her husband's normally reserved countenance was replaced with much happiness and promise for the future. Indeed, the news from Rome that their marriage had been approved by papal bull was cause for even more celebration between the newlyweds. There was no question now as to who the true monarchs were in England.

Thomas had not returned from France, much to Cecily's disappointment. But he had sent several letters to her over the course of spring, asking after her and revealing few details of his mission. Despite her longing for him, Cecily found she was looking forward to the summer's progress when the court would travel to various country houses to visit nobles throughout England. The queen was only allowed to go on progress until the end of June. At that point, she would then need to take up residence at Winchester, where she was to give birth. Cecily was not looking forward to the queen's lying in at Winchester, as they would be placed in the priory, wholly removed from court life and, consequently, Thomas.

She had kept her feelings to herself these long months he had been away. Indeed, the queen asked after him the day he left, but Cecily kept her face neutral, saying she had run into him the night before he had left court and gave him his cloak. Even though she offered no hint of emotion either way, she could feel her friend's eyes on her, searching for the answers surely written all over her face and body.

But no more was said of him until May Day when Cecily's world was turned upside down.

The day had been warm and dry, allowing the court to have a May Day feast in the gardens of Greenwich. Music and dancing swirled around the lawns while a freshly slain hog was making its final turns on the spit. Elizabeth was the Queen of the May Day festivities, and all her ladies had floral crowns woven into their hair. While she did not dance, the queen encouraged her ladies to take up partners and enjoy the music. Through such encouragement, Cecily found herself dancing with a man she had only seen a handful of times. To her knowledge, he was not a frequenter of court.

She made a polite bow as he nodded his head to begin the dancing, and they leaped to the beat of the music in unison with the rest of the dancers. Joining him for one more dance, she found herself breathless and eager for a drink. She said as much, and he led her to the wine fountain and poured her a cup. She took the mug from him, thanking him before she took a long drink.

Breathlessly, he smiled and held out his hand, saying, "I am

Edward, son of the Duke of Nottingham." Cecily grasped his hand and allowed him to place a gentle kiss upon it.

"My name is Cecily. I am a lady-in-waiting to the queen."

He poured himself a mug of wine as well and stood next to her as they watched the dancers.

"Unusual to be participating in such a festive, peaceful affair after all we have been through," he mused, filling the empty space between them. "Have you been with the queen very long?"

"Yes," Cecily replied. "We grew up together."

He nodded. "Much like the king and myself. I was with him from the time he was exiled to Brittany until now."

Cecily turned to look at him, mouth slightly agape. "Then you must know his other friends well, including Thomas."

He laughed and said, "There are many men named Thomas in this country, Cecily, I am sure I know plenty. To which do you speak?" But Cecily didn't know. She didn't know who she was so enamored with, who she had allowed to kiss her, ravish her. She had avoided prying Elizabeth for any answers about him, fearing that it might reveal her desires. Trying to recover, she said,

"I believe he is currently in France as an emissary."

"Oh, that Thomas," he said, laughing. "You would ask about him. Let me guess—dark hair, tall, devilishly handsome and knows it?" Cecily's silence was enough to tell him yes. "Yes, that particular Thomas is near and dear to me. He is my little brother."

Cecily jolted, processing what she had just learned. Thomas had failed to tell her that he was part of the nobility. Indeed, he even lied to her, or at least deflected the truth when they had first talked on the battlements. Looking over his older brother while he kept his gaze on the dancers, Cecily noted that the two shared some similarities. He had the same dark hair, although it wasn't curly. And his skin was also darker than most at court. But his eyes—he did not share his brother's eyes. Nor his brother's height.

Trying to be nonchalant, Cecily asked, "Do you have other siblings?"

"My eldest brother, Eric. You wouldn't have ever seen him. My father likes to keep him close in the north so he can take over the dukedom when he dies. Our father is unwell and is busy settling his affairs."

"I am sorry to hear of it," Cecily said, feeling for all three sons. "Will you return as well to see your father?"

"Not until my brother's wedding later in the summer. I am

needed here, or so I have been told," he said with a glint in his eyes.

"Your father must be pleased to know Eric will be married and his lineage secure."

"Oh, he would like that very much. But Eric won't agree to marrying anyone but his true love. No, it is Thomas getting married." Cecily gasped, unable to control her shock.

"What?" she croaked, her mouth running dry. "He's...betrothed?"

"Nearly seven years now. It's time my brother solidifies it, too."

Cecily's head was spinning, her mind spiraling through flashes of images. His eyes, his delicious grin, his hands holding hers on the battlements, his lips running down her neck, his fingertips dancing between her thighs. His promise to find her when he returned home.

"Are you...all right?" Edward asked, steadying her by her elbow. Cecily closed her eyes and took a deep breath, trying to recover herself.

"It must be the heat and the wine. I think I will go find some shade to sit in."

"Allow me to accompany you," Edward said, seeming sincere.

"No, really, I am just fine. I wouldn't want you to miss out on the festivities." But Edward nonetheless looped her arm into his and said,

"There is a bench just across the other side of the garden that will offer plenty of shade." She allowed him to lead her there.

Once seated, Edward said nothing but kept sipping his wine until his mug was empty. A slight breeze carried the music toward them, reminding her that she should be attending to her queen. But she couldn't fathom smiling and carrying on like her world hadn't slipped out from under her feet.

Edward cleared his throat eventually and said, "Being the middle son, I happen to be a decent listener. I was often a buffer between my brothers and father. So, feel free to say what's bothering you."

Cecily thought, and swallowing hard, she said, "He never told me he was engaged." Edward nodded, urging her to go on without looking in her direction.

"I barely know him, and yet...I thought I knew him so well, too."

"Thomas rarely lets anyone know him."

"I wish I had never met him. My life was perfect before..." she said and sighed. But even saying the words felt untrue. She desperately wanted to know him, but it was all a lie.

"I don't know who my brother is to you, but I can imagine, based on your distress." Silence sat between them again as they watched a pair of doves land on the edge of a fountain just before them. "For what it's worth, he doesn't have a bad bone in his body."

"That is hard to believe for someone in my position," she retorted with a snort.

Edward sighed and said, "Should you two see one another again, I hope you will hear him out." And, as if on second thought, he said more to himself than to her under his breath, "He has always been hopeless with women."

Cecily nodded and said no more. She didn't want to wallow anymore in thoughts of who he could have been to her and who she was or wasn't to him. She hoped she never saw him again— never had to live through the humiliation of him knowing her feelings toward him amidst his lies and how he rendered her completely void of any sense at the touch of his fingertips.

...

Edward seemed to be a fine person in a court where few were decent. Indeed, he had characteristics similar to the Thomas she thought she knew. But that made him all the more untrustworthy in her eyes. And so, as the weeks passed and the court began its summer progress, Cecily did what she could to drive any thought of Thomas from her mind. And on occasions when she was in the same company as his brother, she avoided him altogether. Though Edward did not have those golden eyes of his little brother, his other physical attributes reminded her of him. So, Cecily took it upon herself to evade him at all costs—even sometimes neglecting her duties to be where he was not. She needed time to heal, as silly as it sounded.

...

The court began its progress in early June with visits to various residences along the Thames. But by Midsummer's Eve, King Henry and his court were settled at the Palace of Sheen. This was like a homecoming for the queen and Cecily, as the Palace of Sheen had been one of the places they stayed at as children. The queen's mother, Elizabeth of Woodville, had been granted the palace by her husband, Edward IV. Upon her marriage to the king, Queen Elizabeth's mother bestowed the residence on Henry. Knowing what it would mean to return there before she went into confinement, the king surprised his queen with a large festival in honor of the start of summer.

Elizabeth and Cecily found themselves strolling the garden on the morning of Midsummer. They had only just arrived the night before and were eager to see what had changed since they were last there as girls. They laughed, recalling all the games they played throughout the palace and even contemplated going into the maze. Elizabeth had always been afraid to enter, but Cecily had spent many hours in there, wandering aimlessly while Elizabeth had her lessons. Cecily noted that it was particularly overgrown and likely had not been tended to in several years. But, as Elizabeth remarked, her time for playing in mazes was over because that would be the perfect trap for anyone trying to assassinate the future king of England, or her. Cecily winced at the thought of anything happening to her dear friend and gave a final glance at the maze before moving on to the orchards that sprawled to the edge of the water.

"The bonfire will be set up at the water's edge," Elizabeth said, pointing a finger over to where several dozen men were stacking logs into where the bonfire was set to burn or just next to it to keep it going through the night. "And rather than tables, Henry has insisted we all dine on blankets. He says it is to honor the Solstice, but I have a feeling it just costs less," she said, smirking to herself. Cecily learned through her friend that the king was rather tight with his purse strings.

"Apparently, I am allowed to dance tonight, although my physicians have limited me to three dances. It will be difficult to find anyone to dance with me in this condition," she said, nodding toward her rounded belly.

"You look beautiful, Lizzie. I would have never believed you could be more beautiful than you were on your wedding day, but it appears carrying a king suits you very well," Cecily replied, meaning every word. The queen sighed, grasping her friend's arm as they strolled into the orchards.

"And what of you, dear CeeCee? Anyone you are hoping to dance with tonight?"

"I have no intention of dancing," Cecily replied, meaning it.

"No one has caught your eye yet at this court?" the queen prodded her. Cecily smiled slightly, shaking her head.

"I fear you have never recovered from the loss of Thomas. I wish I had been a better friend in helping you through whatever it was that happened between the two of you."

Cecily recalled how Elizabeth had finally pried her feelings out of her the evening of the May Day ceremony when she had learned from his brother that he was engaged. She had only revealed how the news shocked her but kept the humiliation of being deceived to herself. And also never so much as hinted that she might have behaved very badly with him.

"Well, we better return to the palace to dress for the night. I have a surprise waiting for all my ladies—one I am especially excited about!" the queen said, steering her friend away from the river and back to the palace.

...

"I can't possibly wear this!" Cecily said as she looked down at her dress.

"Yes, you can. We all are wearing something similar. Yours is just...simpler," Elizabeth said with a grin spreading across her face. Simpler was not how Cecily would describe this dress. In fact, there was little to it. How the king's mother would shun them all for their attire. And Cecily said as much to her friend.

"And what of your husband's mother? Will she not be completely offended and...and downright appalled by how little we are wearing?" she asked.

Elizabeth just waved her words away, saying, "She would be appalled by me even if I took vows. You look irresistible, CeeCee, and I want everyone's eyes on you for a change."

Cecily knew her friend meant well, but as she tugged at the dress to get it to cover more of her chest, she knew there was little she could do to change the queen's mind. Elizabeth had it in her head that her ladies-in-waiting should be fair maidens of summer, wearing simple, sheer white gowns that were cut dangerously low on the neckline and had little in the way of fabric between the dress and her skin. Because of the cut of the dress, there was no way she could even wear her shift underneath, which she pointed out to her queen.

"Yes, I thought that might be the case. But it will be so hot anyway. You will be glad for less fabric!" Elizabeth said giddily.

"And speaking of heat, I want each of my ladies to represent an element of summer, and you, fair maiden, will have the crown of fire."

As if planned on cue, the queen's dressmakers knocked at the door and brought in the crowns for each of the ladies-in-waiting. Among the crowns, Cecily noted there was one with ivy, one with flowers, and one with what looked to be songbirds. But the crown of fire was the largest and most eye-catching. And it was breathtaking. It was covered in what had to be thousands of tiny red and gold beads, and it was designed to sit just above her eyebrows and wrap around her head. The dressmaker placed the crown on her head and secured it with several pins and a tie in the back. It was much lighter than she had anticipated.

Elizabeth stood back after it was secured and looked over her friend, admiring her work. "You are devastating. Has anyone ever told you that?"

Cecily felt a small smile pull across her face. "No," she said quietly.

Indeed, no one, not even Thomas, had ever told her that. She found herself slightly more ready to wear the ensemble her queen had put together. And seeing the other ladies-in-waiting filing into the queen's privy chamber to collect their crowns, Cecily was relieved to find she was not alone in exposing most of her bosom to the late afternoon sun shining through the slim windows of the palace.

...

The Midsummer Festival was beyond anything Cecily had ever experienced. Even her distant memories of Yule as a child couldn't compare to the night's revelry. The festival was well underway by the time the queen arrived with her retinue of ladies. Cecily knew it was part of her plan, so her ladies came in just as the sun had set, and she could unleash them in a theatrical display of beauty against the glow of the raging bonfire. As if in a coordinated act, the ladies were instantly swept up by various courtiers, spinning against the firelight. Cecily shared two dances with a prominent nobleman whom she had spoken with a few times. Then she joined another whom she had never met for one final dance before settling on the queen's blanket to watch the dancing.

Cecily drank her wine heartily and then refilled it again. The variety of food was overwhelming, and she picked at various items on the ground before her, savoring the taste of the spiced venison she knew had been taken from the palace grounds before their arrival. Too occupied with the assortment of sweetmeats now set before her, she did not see a man approach her.

"May I have the next dance?"

Cecily spun slowly and saw Edward bowing ever so slightly. She had not expected him to be here nor that he would seek her out. She nodded, and before taking his hand for help off the ground, she gulped down more wine. He tossed her a knowing smirk, but she chose to ignore it.

She had tried to avoid Edward at all costs for fear it would rip open a wound that had started to scab. But as she took his elbow, she surprised herself that she could face him without crumbling into a thousand pieces.

Edward proved to be a pleasant dance partner. He led her with such authority that she didn't have to think about her steps. She even relaxed, and they passed a few pleasantries when they could in between sets. They talked about what he was looking forward to on progress, and she mentioned how she wished she could continue and see more of the countryside. By the end of their third dance together, Cecily found herself laughing as Edward was pointing out which courtiers would end up in the wrong beds that night. He seemed to know much more about the queen's ladies than she did and certainly was in on many scandalous relationships between several married noblemen and their wives.

As he gave her the final spin of the dance, Cecily's eyes caught someone staring at her from across the dance floor. Were it not for Edward's steady grip, Cecily would have stumbled. She would have known those golden eyes anywhere. Edward held her firmly as she regained her footing, never looking away from the eyes piercing her from across the sea of dancers. Edward had seen him, too, and as he bowed to her with the rest of the dancers at the close of the song, he told her something she was not expecting.

"The way I see it is that you have a few choices. I can kiss you here right now and make him realize you have moved on. Or you can hear him out."

Cecily gulped, looking hard into his eyes. She was tempted to take the first offer just to escape. But then she said with irritation, "Or I can ignore both of you."

Edward nodded and replied, "You could. But we both know that you need to hear him out. As much as I would love to claim a kiss from the ravishing Fire Maiden on summer solstice, I know that you should choose option two." And, as though an afterthought, he continued, "And I don't feel like being punched by my brother tonight, either."

Cecily knew she would regret not having closure, so she took a deep breath, nodded and thanked him as he bowed and kissed her hand.

She could already feel Thomas walking toward her as the other dancers realigned with their partners. In the corner of her eye, she saw another man coming to ask for the dance, but Thomas reached her just before him and said with his eyes burrowing into hers, "Hello, Cecily."

She did not reply, instead giving her coldest glare. The music started, and Thomas reached for her hands to begin the dance. She let him hold her, but she knew he could sense her hesitation. As she followed him in the footsteps of the dance, her heart began pounding with fury. How dare he swoop in and treat her as if he were innocent. To act as though he had no reason to beg on his knees for her forgiveness. And yet, as he spun her she was forced to hold his gaze, and he pressed her into his abdomen. She felt her burning passion for him explode within her.

Infuriated, she pushed away from him and left him in the middle of the dance without concern for how it looked to anyone else. As she slipped away from the crowd around the bonfire, she felt her queen's gaze follow her. She knew she shouldn't have dropped her part as the Fire Maiden, but she had to get away from him. She stormed off toward the only place she knew where she could escape everyone's eyes.

Leaving the revelry behind, she slipped into the shadows of the maze. She stopped at its mouth, gasping for cool air, trying to put out the burning of fury and, dare she admit it, desire.

Closing her eyes and leaning against the verdant wall, Cecily did not see him enter the maze. But her eyes snapped open as she felt him there. Looking toward the entrance, she saw his tall figure against the distant orange glow from the fire.

"Cecily."

"Leave me be, Thomas," she said with ice in her voice.

"No," he replied. "I have waited months to see you." Cecily felt a cruel, mocking laugh she had never heard escape her throat.

"I am sure your fiancé would be devastated to hear you talk like that to another woman."

Thomas shook his head subtly. Walking tentatively toward her, he stood on the opposite wall of the maze, keeping a respectful distance between them.

"So that is why you stopped writing back," he said. Once Cecily learned of the betrothal, she threw all of his letters in the fire, never bothering to read them or respond. "I can understand why you are upset." Cecily glowered at his words. "I should have told you, but I didn't know what to make of everything."

"*You* didn't know what to make of everything?" Cecily repeated, her voice still icy. "How hard that must have been for you. Tricking an inexperienced girl into being your plaything while you had someone else lined up to warm your bed." And then, as if the thought dawned on her. "Let me guess, I was not the only one. How can you stand yourself?"

Thomas didn't say anything. Instead, he brushed his hands through his dark, curly hair and blew out a deep breath.

"Would you please hear me out?"

"You could not say anything that would change how I feel about you," she replied coldly.

"Maybe," he said, "but I would be grateful if you would at least know the truth."

Cecily didn't want to give him the satisfaction of swirling reality for her again. And yet, she felt herself rooted to the spot where she was standing. When she didn't move, he began.

"It is true that I am betrothed." Cecily scoffed, looking away from him and toward the opening of the maze. "I have been betrothed since I was seventeen to Margaret. She is the daughter of the wealthiest landowner under my father in Nottingham." And then, as if to step back, he said, "By now, you probably know that I am the youngest son of the Duke of Nottingham."

"Yes, you didn't seem to bother to tell me anything about yourself."

"In fairness, you never asked," he tossed back at her.

"You never gave me the opportunity!" she spat back. But he just sighed and began to pace back and forth in front of her.

"I don't know why I never told you that or avoided telling you that night on the battlements. I guess I liked that you didn't know that about me when everyone else only ever defines me as a duke's son. And so few words were ever passed between us. It just never seemed to come up."

Cecily knew that was true. They had spent so little time together and even less time conversing.

"Being the third son, I am just the second spare in our family tree. And so, to rectify a few bad business dealings and a significant amount of debt that piled up under my father's name during the years of the war, he borrowed money from Margaret's father. When the loan was due, he couldn't pay him back. Some loans were taken to pay for debts to support Henry's war. But I know he also owes for things I don't want to know about, as it will only further scar my opinion of him." He took a deep breath, keeping his eyes on the ground as he paced.

"To extend the loan period and to decrease some of the debt with an advance on her dowry, Margaret's father agreed to marry her off to me. She was nine at the time the arrangements were being made. Now, seven years later, with her being sixteen, we are to marry." Cecily was thus far unimpressed by his story, but something forced her to keep listening.

"Margaret is not...not well," he said carefully. "She wasn't born the way you and I were. While she is sixteen, she will always have the mind of a child. She is incredibly kind and always happy, but she is not..." he paused, trying to find the words. "She is not right. And even though I am to marry her, she will never be a wife to me. I could never do that to her."

But you could do what you did to me without guilt, Cecily thought bitterly. But even as she spoke it in her mind, the fury within her began to dissipate. He stopped pacing and looked at her, searching her face for answers.

"I never told you because, in my mind, I have never been betrothed, not really. And the truth of Margaret being sold off in exchange for debt because she is not quite right is, well, appalling."

"And so you console yourself by making other women your playthings?" Cecily asked, noting that the ice in her voice was melting away.

"No," he replied swiftly. "There has only been you. Recently."

Cecily scoffed at that. "Your brother said you were terrible with women."

He smirked and said under his breath, "Of course he did."

Silence settled between them as he studied Cecily's face carefully. She wore a hardened look, clearly waiting for more answers to justify his deception.

"I have been with other women, it is true. Mostly because I know I will never be truly married to Margaret. But I told myself I would not deceive her, so for several years, I spent more time than I should admit being with other women. But I have never cared for another woman—not until you."

Cecily let his words sink into her.

"I didn't come back to court right away after returning from France because I went home to see if there was any way I could sway my father to release Margaret and me from this betrothal. I even went to her father, asking what it would take to give Margaret the freedom to be who she is without being sold off like an animal at auction. But the truth is, her father is so cruel. And my own father reminded me that if I cared enough to protect her and not dehumanize her the way her own family does, I should be glad to accept her as my wife."

"So you are forced into an impossible decision," Cecily finally said.

"Not really, seeing as the decision is not mine at all."

"No, you are in the same position as Margaret in your father's schemes." Thomas looked at her, intensity in his eyes.

"I went to Nottingham because you were all I could think of in France. I never had hoped for anything with another woman until I saw you, and then...my world flipped upside down."

Cecily's mouth ran dry. That is exactly how she felt. But if she were to chase down all of the memories of the time they spent together, it made no sense. They hardly knew each other. They hardly had spoken. And yet, something had fallen into place for both of them when they met. Something unexplainable, something now impossible, and yet...

Thomas now stopped in front of her and looked into her eyes. She could see her fire crown flashing in his gaze.

"Say something," he pleaded softly.

There were so many things Cecily wanted to say. But what kept running through her mind ever since May Day when she learned about his betrothal was something Edward said.

"Your brother said you didn't have a bad bone in your body." She could tell he was holding his breath, waiting. "I believe you, Thomas."

He blew out the air he had been hanging onto, and then, nodding, he said, "That is all I can ever hope for—that you do not think too badly of me."

Cecily couldn't stand it anymore. With one sweeping step, she closed the distance between them and found herself in his arms. She nuzzled into his chest, holding him as tightly as possible. She could feel the tears squeezing out of her eyes as she drank in his scent, knowing it would never be hers.

He held her until she began to loosen her tight hold of him, and then he pulled her chin up to face him. Wiping her tears with his thumb and kissing her forehead, he said,

"While another may carry my name, you, Cecily, will always carry my heart." And with that, the tears fell more quickly, but rather than letting them slip down her cheek, Thomas began kissing them one by one as they fell.

"I love you, Thomas," she whispered as he kissed her cheeks.

Pulling his lips into a sad smile, he nodded and said, "I have loved you since I first laid eyes on you."

She interlaced her fingers into his and placed their hands between their chests, both quickly rising and falling with their breath, with heartache.

In this moment, Cecily didn't care that he would never be hers. She didn't care that he was betrothed and that she shouldn't be caught with someone who was not, and would never be, her husband. And she decided in a moment that while he would never be hers the way she wanted, she could give him and herself something to cherish for the rest of their days.

Looking hard into his eyes, Cecily lowered their interlaced hands, and she led him into the maze. At first, she walked slowly, but then, feeling the anticipation of what she wanted to do, she started running, pulling him along after her. If the maze hadn't changed since she was a child, she knew exactly where she was going and where she intended to end up.

The center of the maze had a large statue in the middle, but she knew it was visible to anyone peering out of the palace windows facing the Thames. And in tonight's firelight, it would be hard to hide from any eyes remaining in the palace. So, she intended to go to the farthest dead-end corner, which had a secret exit toward the river—a perfect escape if they needed it.

Arriving breathlessly, surrounded by nothing but foliage, a sky full of stars, and the distant sound of music, Cecily pulled Thomas toward her so his hand fell around her waist. Then she grabbed his face, kissing him softly. She ran her fingers through his hair, rubbed her thumbs over his jawline, and pulled his neck closer to hers.

He pressed his hips into hers, shocking her with his already-hardened manhood. Cecily gasped in his mouth, and with a slight moan, she said, "Make me your wife in every way but your name."

He pulled his hips back and looked at her, studying her. "I can't ruin you like that."

"If we get no say in who we spend our lives with, then at least give me this. Give us this," she said, tugging him into her.

And with that, he kissed her hard, lifted her by her buttocks, and wrapped her legs around his waist. He continued to kiss her while he held her standing in that dark corner, their tongues gently exploring their mouths as he turned them slowly in circles. With every brush of her tongue, she sunk into his embrace more until she had to feel more of him—all of him. He gently set her back on the ground and took off his cloak—the cloak she had cradled in her arms every night while it was in her care. He spread it on the grass. Then he knelt down and slipped his hands below her hem to brush her bare feet and ankles. Slowly, his fingers inched up her calves toward her knees, and then, as if to torture her, he walked them further up her leg to her inner thighs.

"You are a goddess," he croaked, looking up at her, the crown sparkling in the moonlight that had just come over the ridge behind the palace. And then, lifting the airy fabric of her dress over his head, he began kissing her bare thighs while she still stood. Her legs weakened as his mouth neared the apex of her thighs, and she sunk down onto his legs, freeing his head from her dress. He held her and kissed her neck softly, then laid her back onto the cloak.

He just stared at her before him, her hair splayed out all around her, the crown still securely attached to her head. To both of their surprise, she began pulling her dress over her knees to encourage him to keep going. He dipped back between her legs and resumed kissing between her thighs. Inching his way to where she wanted his kisses so desperately, he finally arrived, and as he gently nuzzled her with his lips and nose, she arched her back in delight.

Thomas began caressing her delicate skin between her legs with his tongue, causing her to cry out at the delicious warmth that spread from between her legs, up her abdomen, and out her limbs. She wanted to squirm beneath his mouth, but he held her hips firm, causing her to roll her head back and forth to try not to burst so soon. And as she neared her pinnacle, Thomas stopped and crawled over her and kissed her hard on her mouth, the taste of her between them.

Letting her desires be her guide, Cecily rolled Thomas onto his back and straddled him, slowly dropping the sleeves of her gown. Thomas stared at her, drinking in the beautiful drop of her breasts and the petite nipples that beckoned his mouth. But, instead of letting him continue to caress her, she slid back on his legs and began to unlace his breeches. Trying to keep her hands steady, she slowly pulled the ties apart and ran her fingers along the waistband. Thomas sucked in a breath of air at her feather-light touch.

Not wanting to wait any longer, Cecily pulled the breeches down to his knees. His manhood sprung out from the constraints of the fabric, and she couldn't stop staring at him. She had never seen a naked man before and found herself in awe and surprise. She knew what he was supposed to do to her, and yet, she couldn't figure out how something that size would fit into her.

Brushing his length with the back of her fingers, she studied him. Then, she ran her fingertips over the plump mounds beneath him, wonderstruck at the whole image of him. Again, letting her own desires guide her, she settled on the ground between his legs and kissed him on his manhood. He gasped a sharp intake of air and recognizing his response to be the same as her own, she kissed him again, running kisses along the entire length of him. Then she did the same with her tongue, and he let out a growl of pleasure. Feeling her own desire building between her legs, she found herself wanting to lick him more and give him more, but she didn't know what to do next. He pulled her back up to him and kissed her hard, rolling her onto her back.

He sat up between her legs, took off his shirt, and then pulled her dress completely off and tossed it next to them. Covered only by moonlight, Thomas laid his body next to hers, experiencing their nakedness. Cecily twisted her hips so that her buttocks were against his manhood as he lay behind her. She could feel the wetness gathering between her legs, aching for him. He reached his hand around her waist and held her between the thighs, running his fingers slowly over her while drinking in the scent of her neck.

When she could not take any more, she turned back and kissed him, pulling him on top of her. Positioning himself at her opening, he whispered,

"This may hurt, but I will be as gentle as possible."

Cecily nodded into his chest as he separated the silky folds between her legs and pushed slowly into her. She closed her eyes and waited for the pain to come, but all she could feel was her body pulling him into her as though inviting him in. As he pushed further into her, she felt a slight prick of discomfort and took in a sharp breath. He stopped, watching her carefully, but she just tugged his hips closer to her, beckoning him deeper into her. He slid until their hips pressed firmly against one another, and he held himself there, deep within her and kissed her gently on her brow. Then he slowly pulled back and pushed himself back into her. This time, Cecily hardly felt any twinge of pain, and as he continued to do it, she could feel herself relaxing around him. As he pushed in and out of her, he used his free hand to roam all over her body.

He held her breast while he moved inside her, rolling her nipple between his fingers and then slid his hand down her abdomen until it rested between her legs. As he rubbed her silky skin with his fingertips while thrusting into her, Cecily felt the pleasure building inside of her. She wrapped her legs around him, pulling him deeper into her with every thrust. As he leaned down to kiss her forehead, she buried her face in his chest. With his continued rubbing and careful pushes into her, she reached her climax, crying out in pleasure as the warmth of a fire inside her spread all the way to her feet, shooting out of her toes. She felt herself melting beneath him as he quickly slid out of her, spilling his own pleasure onto her abdomen. She watched as his muscles strained with his release, the sweat on his forehead glistening in the moonlight. He then dropped down next to her and wrapped his arm around her the way they had been before he had been inside her.

Cecily's chest was rising and falling quickly, and as she lay next to him, she whispered, "I could do that over and over."

He smiled against her hair and began trailing his fingers down her side and back between her legs. To her surprise, she gasped at the pleasure that was still burning there, and he began to stroke her as he had only moments before. One hand between her legs and the other holding her breast, he coaxed her into another climax. She felt the fire once again ignite within her pelvis and spread throughout her body, forcing her to cry out into his arm that was holding her into his chest. She felt as though she was weightless, floating in the sky like the smoke rising from the bonfire. She had never been more present in her body, yet she was also completely removed from all time or reason as she drifted away in his arms.

"Thank you," she whispered, returning to the solid ground beneath their bodies. She felt his nod, and as they lay together under the moonlight, watching the highest sparks over the bonfire fly into the sky, she wondered at his silence and stillness. Shifting onto her other hip to face him and holding her head up by her hand, she asked,

"Are you all right?" And when he didn't reply, she said, "Thomas?"

He reached up to tuck a strand of hair back into her fire crown, and shaking his head, he said, "No, I am not all right." And, if it weren't for the dancing sparks and moonlight glistening in his golden eyes, she could have sworn tears were floating within them. "I will find a way out of this, Cecily. With everything I am and have, I will find a way. I love you."

"We will find a way together," she said, and pulling him on top of her, she kissed him hard and spread her legs beneath him, drawing him back into her.

4

Elinor's Story

Galway County, Ireland. June 1652.

Cromwell's forces have taken Galway and all surrounding territory. Ireland is falling to the English regime.
Most of the men are dead or away fighting to keep what land is left for Ireland. Meanwhile, women and children are fighting for their lives at home, facing plague, food shortages, and unprecedented changes in laws and regulations.

Like most women, Elinor Acheson has to do whatever she can to keep her family alive. But her fight to feed her family forces her into an impossible circumstance and into the arms of a notorious wolf hunter.

The cold, hard stone of the manor house was pressing into her knees. In that moment, she knew her legs would collapse if it did not cease. Her shoulders were burning, and her neck was on fire. And her jaw—she couldn't think of it. Couldn't focus there. She had gone to the forest in her mind, training her thoughts on the promise that a pine marten would be snared in her trap. Or maybe a hare. Something hearty to bring home to her table that night. The look of joy on her brother's face and the relief on her mother's. One more pump. No, two.

"God, you are a beauty," he murmured, one word per thrust. She willed herself to keep her jaw open.

Finally, the swine groaned with pleasure, spilling his release onto the floor next to Elinor as she wiped her mouth on her dress. The past few weeks, he had been considerate enough to sit and allow her to do the movements, but this time he insisted on thrusting himself into her mouth and took an age to find his climax.

Elinor shakily rose to her feet and waited while he hobbled into his chair behind the ornate wooden desk. She swallowed the urge to spit and wretch at the sight of his pale member hanging limply in his lap. He panted, his eyes closed and his ample stomach rising and falling with every breath. And then, sensing her eyes upon him, he chuckled at the sight of her standing before him, staring down at him. He lazily reached into a drawer, fumbling amongst the contents. His labored movements gave Elinor a few moments to reflect on what he had done to her, bringing about such a level of self-loathing that she wanted to curl up and disappear. But the clang of metal on stone was enough to pull her from her disparaging thoughts. He had tossed a few coins at her feet and leaned his head back into his chair, eyes closed. She quickly scrambled to grab them off the stone floor and turned to escape.

"See you next week, girl," he chuckled behind her back until a heavy cough racked his body. The aged English commissioner was surely getting too old for exertions such as this, she thought bitterly.

Elinor promised herself this time would be the last. She would find a way to feed her family, a way to perhaps escape this part of the country and go somewhere still under Irish control—any other way but receiving him in her mouth. But then she had told herself that every week since the first snow had blown in, bringing with it parliamentarian soldiers who had raided whatever food was left.

Why would this week be any different?

...

As late spring took hold, English parliamentarians began

slowly infiltrating businesses and law in the county. When Thomas Preston, commander of the Irish forces, relinquished the city under siege to the English and fled to France, a tide had turned in the war for freedom. Plague and lack of food and supplies made the residents of County Galway unable to ward off the imposters any longer.

But Elinor's family had survived despite it all. Her mother had even caught the plague, yet she prevailed, though she was a shadow of her former self. Elinor and her brother were left unscathed. Most of their neighbors and friends had not been so fortunate.

Elinor had learned from a young age how to feed herself. Her father used to take her out trapping and fishing, keen to instill his talents for hunting in his only child at the time. She learned how to set her own clever traps, both in the forests and bogs, sometimes catching an otter if she was particularly lucky. Her father even took her on a boar hunt, much to her mother's disapproval. But for Elinor, it had been the most valuable moment of her life. She had learned how to use a bow, and while she did not get to sink the first three blows into the boar, she was able to land the final arrow that caused the beast to fall to the ground. Likely, it was already falling, but her father had insisted she shoot as well, perhaps to give her the courage so that one day if she had to, God willing, she could do it.

But her greatest lessons came from learning how to sniff out and track wolves and where not to set her traps. Her father had warned her that the wolves were cunning and would track her to where her traps were set. In the past few years, they had become such a tribulation that there were rumors that wolf hunters might be unleashed to eradicate the island of the troublesome mutts. In her years trapping and hunting on her own, she had only ever seen tracks and heard the distant howling but had never faced one. Of course, she also never dared to enter deep into the forest where they were known to roam.

When her father left with the other men of her small village to fight in the Irish rebellion, he left her with his traps, his bow and arrow that she would not be able to pull back for almost a decade, and instructions to keep her mother off her feet until her babe was born. For eleven years after her own birth, her mother had been unable to carry a baby beyond a few weeks. But as fate would have it, her father would only learn that he finally sired a healthy, living son days before he was killed in a minor skirmish.

Since that moment of learning her father had died and seeing her mother crumple to the floor with her tiny brother clasped against her chest, Elinor knew her family's survival was entirely dependent on her. And so, she continued to train and hunt. She outgrew her dresses, never owning another one until she was twenty. She learned to braid her long chestnut hair on top of her head so it was never in her way. She tilled the soil so her mother could grow crops. And she learned to barter her pelts and extra meat to buy what they could not take from the land.

And, when Galway was under siege, and there was little food, no supplies, and certainly no coin in civilian hands, she learned a different skill set to make ends meet like so many women before her.

She could still remember the older, weathered woman in the marketplace schooling her in the ways to pleasure a man without taking him. Doing her best to keep the shock from her face, Elinor asked the woman how to trap him, trying to liken it to her hunting. The woman laughed harshly as she looked her up and down. She said it started by dressing like a woman and not a man. And so, Elinor sold six rabbit pelts in exchange for an old, dusty bolt of green fabric that her mother could fashion into a dress for her. Fortunately, her mother finished the dress just days before she fell ill, and Elinor had to put her new skills to work.

She aimed for the biggest prize, as she always did in the forest, and had three different Parliamentarian officers who were all too willing to compensate her for bending her knees. When they left their post for another part of the country, she went for the old commissioner, who she knew was all too willing to pay for these types of services. In the beginning, he gave her more than she had asked. She knew it did not come from a place of generosity.

But, now that the parliamentarians had secured Galway and Irish forces had been pushed out of the county, Elinor was learning that times would only get more difficult for her family. The English hated them, seeing them as barbarians. What they wanted with them and their territory, Elinor could not understand. But she knew she had to get her family out. So when she saw the sign posted in the marketplace a few days after she last visited the commissioner, she found her opportunity for escape.

Wolf Bounty
£6 for female £5 for male
Pelts to be received by Commissioner William Hackney and paid for by the British Parliament.

Elinor had heard of the wolf bounty and the rumors that wolf hunters had infiltrated Ireland on behalf of the English government, which wanted to eradicate them. She had overheard plenty of people in the village complaining about wolves raiding farmsteads and taking what little meat and livestock people had since the siege. Since most landowners were now women, and the men were away fighting or dead, most had no means of defending themselves.

As she walked away from the marketplace, she had already made up her mind.

...

It will be easy, she reassured herself as she stood in their rundown, uninhabited barn, holding the large claw trap in her hands. It couldn't be any different than trying to snare a smaller animal. Other than she would have to leave something to lure the wolf into her trap. And she would have to set it at dusk and go deeper into the forest where she had heard their calling.

The thought of being that far into the forest at night sent a chill down her spine. She could hear her father's words in this very spot before he left to fight. *Never be out after sundown, Eli. You will no longer be the hunter but the hunted.*

She would go that afternoon, she told herself. She would start by scouting out an area where she was pretty certain wolves commonly traversed because the hunting grounds there were aplenty since most people didn't want to venture that far into the forest. She would lay her trap if she found the right spot, but she didn't want to risk it being seen by anyone else.

Wolf hunters were notorious for stealing traps and becoming territorial over certain areas, so she would have to watch for their tracks as well. Most hunted the wolves with dogs and a large group of men on horseback. Going after one on foot, alone, was unheard of unless by accident.

As the sun began its descent in the western sky, Elinor headed out from her home after seeing her brother and mother were well on their way to preparing one of the pine martins she had caught the night before. With another slung over her shoulder and the large claw trap strapped to her back, she snuck around the side of the house without telling them where she was going. Better to not let them worry.

She set a few small traps near her home to catch meat for the next day and then headed in. The forest had never scared her, but it had a way of demanding that every fiber of her was present, listening and looking. After walking well over an hour and leaving a trail of string upon bushes to mark her way in, Elinor had found the spot she wanted to test that night. She had tracked wolf prints into the area and found a clearing in the dense brush and trees just before a stream trickled past. Several hares darted between bushes when she reached the area.

Kneeling down to carefully set the trap and lay her kill next to it, Elinor dusted her hands off on her pants and stood to observe her work. The sun had sunk beyond the trees long ago, and little light was left. Her heart quickened, reminding her she had to get out as quickly as possible. Gathering up what little she had left, she expertly and silently maneuvered through the trees, following the way she came. She had never been so glad to see the candlelight flickering in the windows of her family's stone dwelling when she emerged from the forest.

Rising with the sun the next morning, Elinor left her mother and brother in the bed they all shared. Quietly, she dressed, braided her hair, and grabbed a chunk of hardened, stale bread to quiet her groaning belly on her walk back into the forest. Before leaving, she went into the small barn that had once kept them fed to collect the bow and quiver full of arrows she had hidden beneath a pile of unused straw. She would need it to finish the animal off if there was one snared in her trap.

Elinor snuck back into the forest with the bow and quiver strapped to her back, keeping her feet as light as possible as she finally neared the clearing. Her ears were piqued for any sounds of boars, as they often roamed early in the morning after the wolves had prowled at night. Slowly peering around a tree where she could get her first look at the trap, her spirits dropped. Nothing.

Sighing with disappointment, she went to collect her trap. As she neared the spot, she took a sharp inhale, seeing that her kill had been taken. Being mindful of her footsteps, she studied the dirt around her feet. *One was here.* Although barely visible in the hard-packed earth, the peaks of dirt between the pads were fresh and undisturbed. And no rabbits were rustling between the bushes this morning, so they must have been scared off by the predator.

Elinor weighed her options. She could come back and reset it tonight and try again. But she felt the outcome would likely be the same. And then she realized she had made an amateur mistake. The trap was barely concealed, so, of course, the wolf would avoid it. In her desperation to set the thing and be done last night, she hadn't considered hiding it out of plain sight. Frustrated with herself, she resolved to set the trap in some low brush with a dead animal next to it. She decided to risk leaving it out during the day and hid the trap in some thick brush, then she left to check her other traps.

To her disappointment, yet again, only one hare was caught the night before. Should she feed it to her family or use it to try to lure the wolf? She grappled with what she should do the rest of the way home. But, when she arrived at the cottage to see her brother digging for worms in the once-productive garden, she had an idea to take him fishing. She quickly skinned the hare and placed it in her mother's grateful hands to prepare. Before she turned away, her mother brushed away a loose tendril of hair from her braid and said,

"Whatever would we do without you, Eli."

She tried to brush off the statement, but Elinor's greatest fear was, indeed, what would happen to them if she were not there. Being only nine and incredibly scrawny, Conor was still too young to hunt on his own, and her mother had remained so weak after the illness. Even if she were healthy, crops didn't keep with soldiers raiding gardens at any time of day, and few people had farm animals these days due to the pillaging and slaughter. She had seen a few hens for sale at the market. If she was luckier with her traps that night, she might be able to save up to buy one or two for the eggs—something they hadn't had in months.

Elinor resolved to start teaching Conor the basics of trapping in case anything should ever happen to her. As they walked to one of the many estuaries feeding the land from the sea, she explained the basics of how to find the right place to set a trap and how to track small game. While they walked, Elinor pointed out various prints in the dirt. Conor proved to be a good pupil, and by the time they reached the sea, he had correctly identified each of the small animal tracks Elinor had introduced to him.

Conor was a quiet boy. As he brushed away the curly black hair blowing in his eyes with the wind coming off the sea, Elinor's heart wrenched, as it often did, when she would yet again realize that he would never know their father. How lucky she had been to have what years she did with him.

Between checking the lines every so often, he passed the time by scraping a stick in the sand.

"What are you drawing?" Elinor asked, sitting down in the sand next to him.

"Nothing in particular," he said, his voice muted by the wind.

"Has Mother taught you to write your name?" He shook his head, the hair falling back in his face.

"Here," she said, picking up a stick beside her.

Writing his name in the sand, she beckoned him to trace her letters with his stick. He then practiced on his own, a small smile pulling across his face as he finally finished. Elinor matched his smile, but she couldn't quiet the guilt that surfaced in her as she noted how little she or her mother had been able to give him. There were hardly any other children his age to play with as most families moved away before the siege. And they had been one meal shy of begging for so long that neither she nor her mother had anything left to give outside of finding food.

Tossing her stick into the sea as he continued to trace his name in the sand next to her, Elinor resolved to stop at nothing to get as much money as she could from the wolf bounty.

That afternoon she taught Conor to gut the fish they caught before taking it to their mother. He was so eager to learn and clearly thrived in being useful. As she was gathering up her trapping supplies, he begged her to come. She looked into his bright green eyes, seeing the need there, but she gently shook her head and placed her calloused hand on his shoulder.

"If you can keep a secret from Mother," she said, kneeling down to be eye level. "I have to go deep into the forest tonight. I can't risk having to worry about you and trying to keep myself safe, too. Do you understand?"

He looked at her, disappointment washing over his face. But then his eyes grew wide, and he said,

"You're not going after something big, are you, Eli?"

She hesitated, and then, standing, she said, "No, not something big. I will be perfectly fine. You will see." She gave his shoulder an extra squeeze, gathered up the remnants of the fish that she had subtly wrapped in leaves, and headed toward the forest.

Good to her word, Elinor was fine and returned well after dark. She felt much surer this time that she had laid an irresistible path right into the metal claws of her trap. The stink of the fish alone would surely draw wolves to the place.

But to her disappointment, her trap was left empty once again. Yet, the fish guts had been taken, and paw prints circled the trap. Elinor leaned against a tree, trying to keep from throwing herself against it in frustration. Her belly was gnawing with hunger as there had been nothing to eat this morning. The thought that Conor and her mother would feel the same pains devastated her. At least they had eaten well the night before. She would have to go back to the commissioner tomorrow. Tears began to swarm the bottom of her eyelids as she wracked her mind for a better way to entice the creature.

Looking up to blink the tears away, she found herself staring at a thick, mossy, low-hanging limb. If she jumped, she could graze it with her fingertips. It sparked something in her, causing her mind to race with possibility. A wolf was clearly here two nights in a row and would likely expect more food to be there tonight upon its return. The problem was not luring the wolf here. The problem was catching it. She could try laying the food on either side of the trap, but to miss it another night was not an option. The pressure of the bow and quiver on her back was confirmation enough that this branch was the only way.

...

Returning to the clearing just before sundown, she carefully laid her trap concealed by sticks and leaves she had gathered around the perimeter. Last night, she had only caught one hare again in her traps near home. She left the legs for her mother to cook for her and her brother for dinner while she picked a handful of berries on her way into the forest. Elinor took the remaining carcass and sliced it down its middle to release the fresh scent of meat. She left it as an offering in the middle of the clearing. Then, she made for the tree she had stood against early that morning. As she did so, she could have sworn she was being watched. A prickle ran up her spine as she scanned the perimeter around her, but she detected nothing.

Pulling a rope out of her pack, she slung it over the thick branch and used it to help her climb up the tree. She had always felt strong from the miles and miles that she walked every day, but she did not welcome the weakness she felt in her arms as she pulled herself and her pack up. Finally hoisting herself onto the branch, her skin stinging from the bite of the bark, she tried to create a perch for herself leaning against the tree. Settling on her pack to soften the hard seat, she took the rope, wrapped it around her waist, and tied it against the branch. Should she fall asleep or lose her balance when the time came, she would have something holding her in place. Lastly, she slung her quiver over a protruding knot in the trunk near her head and nocked one arrow in her bow.

Now, all she had to do was wait. Wait and try not to think

about the groaning in her belly, the ache of hunger in her throat, or the blow of what it would be to have to kneel on those hard stones tomorrow. But mostly, to try not to fear what would happen to her body if she missed her shot and the wolf instead found her.

Elinor had never been afraid of the forest, but being strapped to a tree all night long was a level of vulnerability she had never experienced and not one she was eager to experience again. Every rustle in the bushes, each flutter above her head, a distant call of an owl—any sound or indication of movement—sent her heart racing. And she couldn't ignore this ever-present feeling that she was being watched. She just prayed it wasn't the wolves stalking her.

At some point, rabbits had started bounding around the clearing, forcing Elinor to relax her muscles. If the rabbits were active, there was little threat. She even may have dozed off for a bit, having no recollection of how much time had passed, but the ache in her neck told her she had not so much as moved a muscle for a considerable length of time. Focusing her eyes on her surroundings again, she realized the rabbits were no longer moving. The forest, indeed, had gone entirely still. Elinor was sure if anything was out there, it would hear her heart pounding against her chest.

And something was there. Just shy of the clearing, Elinor could see its shape take form. The wolf was here. She silently flexed her fingers before grasping the bow properly and checking that her arrow was perfectly nocked. As she did so, the animal sauntered toward the carcass and sniffed around it. She knew it was picking up her own scent. And, as if to confirm this, the wolf looked toward the base of the tree she was sitting in. Her blood ran cold. She knew a wolf could get her from her perch—it would be difficult but not impossible. But, as though dismissing the notion that a human was here, the wolf turned back to the meat and quickly clamped it in its jaws and made to turn back the way it came.

No, don't go that way! And, as if her silent plea was answered, the wolf suddenly stopped, perked up its head to listen, and darted back through the clearing right in front of her. Elinor raised her bow and made to draw back the strings, but even in her own swift movement, she knew she had no chance. Before the disappointment could flood her, the bushes rustled, and three more wolves bounded into the clearing.

They were smaller than the first wolf, and they were sniffing the perimeter of the clearing. The smallest wolf sniffed all around the concealed trap and then stilled its body as it perked up its ears to listen. Its flank was perfectly exposed to Elinor. Now was her chance. Before she could fight down the fear that had enveloped her body, she drew back the bowstring and aimed her eye down the wooden arrow. She wanted to let it release right away, just to be on the other side of this moment. But she heard her father's voice in her head, the memory of his gentle hand on her shoulder as she had stared down the boar. *Always take a deep breath before you release, Eli.* She did so and, with her exhale, she let go of the string, keeping her body perfectly still to help guide the arrow into its target.

A yelp erupted from the wolf as the blow from the arrow knocked it onto its hip. She had hit it in the abdomen—just right of her target. The wolf tried to stand and follow the others as they ran off yipping through the forest. Elinor quickly drew another arrow and this time fired it into its shoulder. The beast fell completely this time, yelping all the while. Elinor drew another arrow and fired it, wholly missing her target by sending it straight into the ground near its head. The animal kept trying to stand, but it was too wounded. She reached for her fourth arrow, and this time, she bought herself two breaths before sending the killing blow between the ribs into the wolf's heart.

Its body shuddered for several minutes as it bled out, and then a stillness washed over the whole forest. Elinor leaned her head back against the tree, the rush of the moment causing her to shake all over. She had done it. And as she used her breath to settle her beating heart, she couldn't help but feel that she was still being watched.

...

The next day, she walked her usual path to the commissioner's manor house at the top of the village. But this time, she was not donning her dress. Nor was she walking with a cloud of shame over her head. This time, she marched with her head held high wearing her hunting clothes with the wolf's grey tail in her hand.

There was some part of her that felt desperately sorry for having to slay such a beautiful animal. When she had crouched next to it in the forest where it was slain, she laid her hand on the thick grey hair, admiring the magnificence of such a creature. As her hand rested on its body, her fingertips tingled as she grazed the wolf's fur.

She did not make eye contact with anyone in the market, even those she often bartered with. While she could not hide her pride from herself in what she had accomplished in the early hours of that morning, she knew that most would not take kindly to a woman going after wolves. And she also felt a stir in their whispers, no doubt questioning how she came to carry such a thing.

Even though her mission here was completely different, she still felt an overwhelming sense of dread entering the commissioner's house. His assistant looked her up and down with a quizzical eye when she approached his desk just outside the study doors. Then his eyes settled on the wolf's tail, and his face widened in disbelief.

"Not here on personal business then, today?" he said, amusement in his tone.

"No," Elinor replied, trying to keep her head high.

"You will need to wait then until he can see you." She nodded and turned to lean against the stone wall while the assistant slipped into the office.

But she did not have to wait. The commissioner himself came out to greet her.

"What a surprise to see you like *this*," he said, a smirk on his face and his eyes bright with amusement as he looked her up and down. "I had to come out to see it with my own eyes. My previous visitor just told me a rumor was circulating that a village girl was carrying a wolf's tail."

His eyes now settled on the tail clutched in her hand. She saw a slight grimace pass over his face as he took in the bloody remnants of the spinal cord waving beneath the furry length.

"So," he said loudly, finally pulling his gaze away from the tail or perhaps her breeches. "Where is the rest of the beast?"

"At home," she said. He clicked his tongue, still taking her in.

"And you will be wanting payment now, I presume?"

"Yes," she said firmly. The commissioner smirked, running his hands over his protuberant belly.

"Yes, you always like to be paid right away," he mused, walking closer to her now. "And you have a permit?"

"A what?" Elinor asked, her mouth running dry.

"A permit, girl. To hunt wolves in Britain, you need special approval by way of a permit stating you have permission to hunt these lands."

Elinor stared at him and then said quietly, "The notice said nothing of a permit."

"Yes, well, it's a rather new enforcement now that domestic matters are no longer under Irish control. An attempt to bring you all out of your barbaric ways," he said, amused. And then, as though an afterthought, "Of course you would know that if you attended the town halls, but you can't because you are a woman."

Elinor's eyes blazed at him, fury starting to cloud her vision. None of the villagers could go to the meetings because most were women or elderly men who couldn't leave home. Therefore, the citizens had no voice in any matters pertaining to regulations.

He studied her carefully and spoke to his attendant without removing his gaze from her. "Please take the horses and cart and go to Miss Acheson's house to collect the wolf. She and I will settle the matter while you are gone."

Elinor studied him as he rose up and down on his toes in anticipation of what he was going to demand of her.

"The wolf is hidden," she blurted out as the assistant started walking toward the heavy wooden doors.

"Is it now?" the commissioner grinned, drawing closer to her now. She could smell the familiar scent of tobacco, sweat, and something slightly putrid coming off him. "Is it really hidden, pet, or have I caught you in tricking us, Miss Acheson?" His lips drew back further, revealing the black-stained teeth normally hidden behind his thick grey facial hair. She met his gaze with a hard glare.

"It is in the barn beneath the straw. I will go with you," she said through gritted teeth, nodding toward the assistant. And as she made to walk away, he snatched at her arm and brushed her cheek with the backs of his roughened fingertips.

"You will go with him, but you must come back to collect your money." His eyes glimmered. She knew what he was asking for. And she knew she would yield to him in fear that if she did not, he may not pay her at all for not having a permit.

Upon her return with the assistant, Elinor felt the stares of nearly everyone in the marketplace as their cart carried the slain wolf in the back of it. Whispers were circulating even more now. And as predicted, when she returned, she followed the commissioner into his office and kneeled behind his desk.

"Next time, you will dress accordingly," he said as he thrust his limp member into her mouth. "Or else, I won't be so forgiving."

She let him drive himself in and out of her mouth for longer than it had ever taken him until he sagged with relief. Then she rose to tower over his weakened figure in his chair. Cool fury lifted her off of her knees.

"And next time when I bring you another wolf, I will again show you my gratitude for turning another blind eye to the fact I do not have a permit." She would do anything to get the money she needed to help her family escape, even if it meant coming here two more times. Then she grabbed the pouch of coins he had set on his desk for her and strode out of the room, trying not to run.

...

When she killed her second wolf two nights later, Elinor finally started allowing herself to feel excitement for the future. Never before had she given herself such a luxury, but she began making plans. She had earned twelve pounds by slaying two female wolves, and she knew there was still another female in their pack and a male who had been there the first night. She told herself she needed just one more wolf to buy their freedom. Her plan was to ferry to a remote village in the northwest corner of Ireland where her father's cousin had a farmstead. Elinor had received a letter from him and his wife offering them residence when news spread across the country about the siege of Galway.

Her mother and Conor had found out about what she had

done the same day as she collected on her first wolf. Their neighbors had caught wind of rumors from town. Some of them were not so forgiving.

Her mother, who rarely had the energy to squeak out a "Good morning" or "fetch some water," found it in herself to shout—actually shout—at Elinor for her recklessness. Elinor had been near tears at the sight of her mother's anger toward her, but she held her chin high and told her the plans she was making for their family. Her mother then went silent and hadn't spoken to her since that outburst. Elinor knew leaving would be devastating for her mother, as she had grown up in Galway. But nothing was left for them here except starvation, as Elinor gently reminded her before her mother turned away to curl up in their bed. She tried to quiet the nagging voice of bitterness in her head that her mother had no idea what she had done already to keep them alive.

Conor, on the other hand, was livelier than ever. He wanted to know everything about how she had slain the wolf and even asked if he could come with her the next time. Elinor ruffled his hair and spent the afternoon teaching him how to fire a bow and arrow with the one her father had fashioned for her at that age.

When she came to town to turn in her second wolf, she borrowed a cart from their neighbor to haul it. Upon reaching the commissioner's manor, she was told to wait outside until he was ready for her. It was all she could do to ignore the staring faces walking past her. One mother had pulled her child away as they walked past Elinor. She laughed to herself about how she must look in her dress, leaning next to a wolf carcass, picking her nails with a knife. Elinor had chosen to change into her dress so the commissioner had no reason to withhold payment, especially when she was getting closer to her goal.

After several minutes of silent scrutiny from the townspeople, the doors to the manor finally flew open, and the assistant beckoned her inside. Two men she had never seen came out to haul the carcass inside the building. Elizabeth walked into the entryway, and the commissioner's face paled at the sight of her.

"Another one, then, girl?"

She nodded. He looked befuddled, which was unusual for him. He turned into his office, beckoning her to follow. Elinor swallowed hard, anticipating what she would have to do next.

But to her surprise, he pointed toward the only other chair in the room, inviting her to sit down while he took his own seat. With one hand pulling at his overgrown eyebrow and the other tapping on his armrest, he finally said,

"How did you get it this time, Miss Acheson?"

"Same as last. Arrow through the heart."

He looked up, studying her.

"I feel I should warn you, girl. Wolf hunters have moved into the area. You would do well to stay out of their way now."

"Am I not a wolf hunter, too?" she said with a slight smile creeping across her face. He laughed, although it was strained.

"I won't deny my surprise at your ability to kill not only one but two wolves. But, like I said, you would do well to keep out of their way. Especially the one who has moved into Aughnanure Castle. He has actually just paid me a visit, and is, well, not to be crossed." He continued to pull at his eyebrow, his thoughts apparently still consumed by his last visitor.

"He will not like to know a woman is slaying his wolves, so it is best we keep these two between us. And you will get no more. Do you understand me?" His cold grey eyes stared at her across the desk. She matched his stare, words escaping her. He smirked, and then, standing again from his chair, he walked around his desk and leaned on the edge of it in front of her. She did not miss his intention.

Reaching up to stroke her cheek with his crepey, pale hand, he said, "You will not find these men as...accommodating as I have been, pet."

He pulled his finger down her lip. And then his urgency overcoming him, he began to fumble with his breeches. Disgust and revulsion rose up in her throat like bile as he beckoned her to begin with a nod of his head. Every fiber of her body was reeling, screaming at her to not give in. She just stared at him, searching for a bargain. She needed one more kill. And even though she would rather be surrounded by wolves alone in the dark forest at night than allow him to defoul her mouth, she reminded herself she would do whatever it took to get her family out of Galway.

"Let me get one more," she said, lowering herself out of her chair to her knees, trying to give him an encouraging smile. His breath caught between his blackened teeth as he bared them at her. Thrusting himself toward her face, he groaned and said, "Get on with it, girl." And she did, hoping he would recognize her sacrifice in the bargain.

After he finished forcing himself into her mouth, he leaned back onto the desk, groaning with discomfort from the strain in his legs. She stood quickly, the chair scraping out from underneath her. She reached out for her payout, and he obligingly set it into her hand. Without a word, she turned away and began to make for the door. But as her hand reached the handle, he said,

"No more wolves, Miss Acheson." Elinor turned back, gaping at him, words lost behind the wall of fury that had risen within her. He detected it and sneered at her dismay. "You bring me another one, and I will notify the powers above me."

She balked at him. Finding her words, she blurted out, "But you're the commissioner. You are essentially the government here."

His shoulders drew higher as she said this. But then he said, "It is no longer my decision. It's out of my hands."

"Then who do I speak to?"

He looked at her bemused and said, "I promise you, girl. You do not want to ask any favors of these men."

"Who do I speak to?" she pressed, emphasizing each word slowly so as to convey how serious she really was.

He studied her for some time, a glint in his eye.

"Captain Everard. A member of the Cromwellian forces. High up in rank from what I hear. And a wolf hunter. Not one to cross. I hear he killed a wolf with his bare hands," he paused, letting the words sink in. "He is in charge of the wolf bounty now. Good luck finding him and pleading your case."

Satisfied to at least have a name, Elinor turned to walk away.

"And don't come back here again. I don't want people associating me with you amid the rumors that you have caused." And, as if to deliver the final blow, he sneered, "It wasn't that good anyway."

She should have felt relieved at being released from having to service him. But the need for one more wolf, one more chance to get enough money for passage out of this place, consumed her mind. She would find this captain and would go so far as to become part of his hunting troop if she had to.

Had she not been so preoccupied with getting one last wolf, she would have wondered what rumors were being spread about her.

...

As Elinor loaded her pack that night, fury still coursed through her veins about the commissioner yet again forcing his way into her mouth, the bounty being taken away from the villagers, and the hurdle of finding one more wolf without guarantee of payment. She knew how to lure the wolves, and now, she would take one last one and find a way to get her money from the captain himself.

Before she walked into the belly of the forest that night, she told her mother to start packing up the house and readying to leave. Her mother had looked at her wide-eyed when she held out her hand with twelve pounds in it. With no words for her daughter beyond a nod of her head, she gave her daughter a soft embrace and stroked her cheek before heading into the house. Elinor turned to Conor and told him to help their mother and that she would be back at sunrise.

Walking away from the cottage, her feet were swift on the ground, carrying her one last time before she hopefully freed them from this land. As she trudged her usual route to the clearing, Elinor tried to dismiss this intruding feeling of being watched. *It's just the small creatures.* She often sensed eyes were on her, but the past few nights in the forest had felt different.

Once she reached the clearing, she sensed an unusual silence settle in the forest, causing her ears to roar. Pushing against her instincts, she laid her kill right in the center of the cleaning, not bothering with a trap this time. She had been lucky overnight and had caught several small animals, all of which she laid to lure the male wolf into her lair.

She then climbed her usual tree and settled as she had the previous nights. She did not expect the wolf to come until the early hours of the morning, so she rested her head back and thought of all she would need to prepare to take on the journey to the north. Fortunately, they had so little, there wouldn't be much to take. The hardest things to leave behind would be her father's traps. He had entrusted them to her—as though he knew she would one day need them to keep their family alive. She would sell them at the market and use what they got for them to help set up a new home. As for the rest of the house, she planned to open it up and let the neighbors pick over what furnishings they had. She knew now was no time to be greedy and that the villagers were just as hungry as her family had been.

Elinor's thoughts of who she would invite first to look over their possessions were suddenly halted by a distant thundering of steps. Something large was tearing through the forest, getting louder the longer she listened. The steps were soft, and yet there were also new sounds that she had not heard in the forest. Her heart pounding in her ears, she raised her body to crouch on the thick tree branch, lifted her bow, and nocked her first arrow. She took a deep breath. She could tell the animal was running, and if she had any chance, she would have to kill it the moment it emerged in the clearing.

With the noise thundering down on her, a rush of branches parted as a large wolf erupted out of the foliage and into the clearing. Without a beat, Elinor let her arrow fly. She felt no hesitation this time. The yip of the animal sliding into the dirt on contact signaled her to prepare her next arrow. She drew back and fired again, and as she did so, three men on horseback emerged out of the same path that the wolf had been on.

Elinor froze. Her legs cramped as she remained kneeling on the tree branch, trying not to move a muscle. The huge, dark rider at the head of the pack quickly slid down his horse while it was still slowing and ran to the beast, knife in hand. He knelt down next to it as it fought to get to its feet. But as the man knelt beside it, the animal's muscles stilled, save for its ragged breathing. In one swift motion, the man slit the wolf's throat, its body shuddering with relief. The air stilled around them as the man stayed beside the wolf, placing a hand on its chest. Several moments passed. And then he turned and looked over his shoulder. Right at her.

The stare that sliced the air between them was like an arrow to her own body. Never had she seen such cold fury. Elinor didn't know the last time she had taken a breath, yet she found the strength to stand up on the tree branch, bow still clutched in her hand. She matched his stare with what she hoped was an equal coldness. She took note of his black leather clothes, the pants so tight it was as though they were painted onto his body. Long black hair coated with sweat hung next to his tanned face. From her vantage point, he had no weapons on him save for the glimmering, etched knife in his hands.

Still under his cold gaze, she slung the bow over her back next to her almost full quiver and slid down from the tree. He rose next to the wolf as she landed firmly on her feet, her thick chestnut braid falling down to her waist. She made her way toward him.

As she drew closer, her eyes had to shift upward to hold his gaze. He was massive. She only came up to his chest. Seeing how large he was made the fear well up in her body, but she tried not to let her gaze falter. She wanted to say something bold, something with strength, but it was as though he muted everything in her.

Instead, he said darkly, "I've been waiting for this moment."

Her heart pounded, the sweat pooling in the crevices of her fist still clutching the bow. His voice was low, almost like a growl, the eyes now bright blue when she could've sworn they were the color of storm clouds—of metal—when he first saw her.

"You must be the wolf hunter that has taken away our rights to hunt," she said coldly. He pursed his lips, letting the realization of who he was sink into her. His eyes never left hers. When he didn't say anything, she said, "This is my wolf."

Separating his legs to stand squarely in front of it, he growled, "This wolf belongs to no one."

And, as if on cue, the two other riders with him, both almost as tall and fierce and dressed just the same, slid down their horses and made their way to the wolf. From behind him, the two men gathered up the body and carried it back to the horses, slinging it carefully over the back of one of them.

"I killed it!" she nearly shouted through her gritted teeth, pointing in the direction of the slain animal.

"Yes, you did," he said coldly. "But it will not be going home with you." And then his eyes narrowed in on her. "And you will not be going home either."

Elinor made out to scream for help, but no sounds escaped her mouth as he quickly picked her up and carried her through the clearing toward his horse. She kicked and eventually gutted out a piercing scream, all while still in his arms. He only held her tighter. An owl and several birds flew out of distant trees, their wings beating against the silence that settled after her scream.

Her final attempt to free herself was to bite the massive fore-arm that clutched her body to his. He inhaled a sharp breath at her bite, but rather than getting angry or withdrawing in pain, he merely sent out a deep laugh and set her on his horse, tossing her bow and quiver to the man on their left. He caught them with one hand. Slinging his leg onto the horse and settling his hips behind hers, he wrapped his thick arms around her to clutch the reigns. Pinned against him, she gave in, knowing that she would never win in this fight at this moment. She had to save up her strength in order to survive. Now, she just had to see where she would be taken.

With a subtle nod of his head to his men, her captor rode off through the clearing, the two other riders flanking them. As they rode past the tree where she had hunted from, Elinor could have sworn she saw herself still crouched there, watching herself ride off with the huntsmen.

A haunting thought came over her—she would never return from his imprisonment. And she would never be the same.

...

They rode for what felt like an eternity, but since the sky was completely black, it still had to be night, and they couldn't have gone too far. Were it not for the fear shrouding her, the sway of the horse's back would have lulled her to sleep. How long had it been since she had truly slept at night without fearing for their lives, for her mother and brother? And then, as her mind screamed out to her to do something for them, to fight for them, she said quietly in the dark of night,

"I have a family to care for."

"I know," he said, all too casually.

"You are cruel."

"That I also know." Elinor's ears were burning with rage.

"They will starve without me," she said through gritted teeth.

"No, they won't," he said simply.

Elinor wanted to smash the back of her head into his face, but he was so much taller it would just hit him square in the chest, and she would be the one who was hurt. She fell silent again, consoling herself with the fact her mother had the money she had made on the other two wolves in her hand. It could buy them time while she was wherever she was going.

A distant flickering of lights came into view. Towering against the dark sky was a stronghold with a tall tower. As they neared, she saw that the tower was six windows high—with each window glowing from the firelight within. From her vantage point, it looked as though the fortress was impenetrable. Not that anyone would try to find their way in for her.

As the foreboding tower approached, the horses waded through a small river just next to it, emerging out of the forest and onto the ground of the stronghold. Elinor's mouth ran dry. It looked like the type of place where one would be held prisoner, which she now realized was what she was.

The rider behind her urged his horse through the gates that had been left open for them, and they entered the courtyard. Several dogs were barking all around them, greeting their masters. The man halted the horse and slid down swiftly, the horse moving beneath her legs as it adjusted to the lighter weight on its back.

Without a word to her, he went over to the rider with the wolf's body slung across it and picked it up in his arms. Carrying it across the courtyard, he walked toward a long table covered with straw, which was also spread out below. The other riders now came up to him. They were discussing something when, finally, they looked over in her direction, and those icy blue eyes settled on her face. Nodding, he walked toward her while the other two stood guard over the wolf, and he lifted her down from the horse as though she were a small child. Grabbing her upper arm, he steered her through the courtyard and to the entrance of the tower. She flung her arm to release his grip from her, and he surprisingly let go.

She turned up to his face, and he looked at her. A hint of amusement crept across his face. Then, with the hand he had released from her, he beckoned her to lead the way through the doorway. But she didn't move.

"Where are we?" she demanded.

Retracting his outstretched hand, he replied, "Aughnanure Castle."

"Why?"

He cocked his head to study her, his long hair slipping in front of his eyes.

"Because I live here."

"How wonderful for you," she said sarcastically. "But why am *I* here?"

"Consider yourself under arrest for the time being." Her blood ran cold.

"For what?" she asked firmly.

"For slaying wolves."

"My family is hungry."

"They were not yours to take."

"And they're yours to slay?" Fury was bubbling up inside of her. Pointing her finger at him, she said, "Just because you are English does not mean that everything on this island is yours for the taking. You do realize that people lived and hunted here long before your people set eyes on us?"

She could tell she had struck a note because he looked daggers at her, and his fists were clenching at his side. *Good, may he hate me as much as I hate him and his people.* But she wasn't done.

"You wolf hunters are pathetic, you know that? Hunting these animals down with your packs of dogs instead of taking them on single-handedly. You are all cowards. You're *weak.*" She spat at his feet.

Fury rose up in his eyes like a curtain, turning them metallic. Elinor's breath caught in her throat at the sight of the shift. He grabbed her arm hard and pulled her through the doorway, a lit entrance hall, and up six winding sets of stairs. They had passed no one. By the time he reached the top floor, her arm was burning with his grip. She wanted to cry out in pain, but she refused to show him any weakness. Arriving at the only door on that level, he threw it open and stood aside, pulling her into a room. His chest was panting, not with exertion—with rage.

"This is where you will stay," he growled. "You will be unharmed, clothed, and fed. No man will cross this threshold. But you will not leave until you are invited to." Elinor's jaw dropped in protest.

"And what if I do?" she growled back.

He stared at her—his silver eyes flickering in the moonlight. She could have sworn something gave in him, just a little, at her defiance. But his next words were as cold as ice.

"If you leave, I will hunt you down." And he shut the door without another word, his footsteps echoing throughout his entire journey back down the steep climb from where she was now imprisoned.

Elinor's feet finally gave way as she sunk into the reality of where she was. Crumpled on the floor, she let tears of rage and fear soak the wooden planks next to her feet. Whispering out a plea for help, she said through ragged breaths,

"I only wanted to save my family."

Eventually, the exhaustion and the darkness forced her body to give into sleep.

...

Elinor had no recollection of climbing onto the large, canopied bed the night before. But laying on top of the covers with a thick woolen blanket over her still fully clothed body, she had an unsettling feeling that someone had put her there. And had taken the liberty of removing her wet boots. The scent of pine and woodsmoke slowly pricked her memory.

She sat up quickly, her heart immediately racing as the realization of where she was hit her. She was in a castle farther away from her home than she had ever been. And she was a prisoner. Elinor leaped toward the small window and looked down into the courtyard they had passed through in the early hours of the morning. There was little activity beyond a few hounds scrounging around in the dirt. Yet the sun had already risen well above the trees. Her mother and Conor must be frantic, she thought—or at least hoped.

Pulling on her boots and lacing them quickly, she lunged toward the thick wooden door. But when she placed her hand on the handle, she halted. Of course, it would be locked. No one would leave their prisoner in an unlocked cell. But she tried anyway, and when the lock gave way and the door creaked open, her jaw dropped. No one was guarding her on the landing. And no one was keeping her in. She did not hesitate as she started walking down the stairs. She passed no one, but as she neared the second-floor landing, she heard voices coming from the first floor. Elinor had no idea of the layout of the house, as she was too preoccupied with fighting the wolf hunter off when she was brought in. But now, she regretted not having looked around. If only she knew what rooms surrounded the entrance.

As she quietly stepped down the final set of stairs, she saw there was only the entrance hall with a few rooms jutting off on either side. She paused as she was nearly on the last step to listen.

She hadn't heard the other men speak last night, but she assumed it was their voices she was hearing from what she thought might be the dining room. She waited for the deep voice she associated with the wolf hunter, but it never came. From the other side of the hall was a clang of pans in what had to be a kitchen. So both sides of the entrance hall were occupied. She landed on the last step and turned slowly to peer behind the stairs. There was a door almost as large as the one in front of her leading into the courtyard. She remembered from last night that the castle appeared narrow. Perhaps this was another exit. If she went straight, she would certainly run into someone—perhaps a guard or, at the very least, attract the attention of the men in the dining room. But if she went behind the stairs, she might have a chance.

To her relief, no one saw her, and the door opened without a sound, revealing the back of the tower. The stables were kept there, as were what looked like empty servants' quarters. Elinor kept near the wall and followed it around to where she believed there might be an exit. But seeing as the castle was a stronghold for whoever had lived here before these men had moved in, it appeared the only possibility was going straight through the entrance. If she overthought it, she would come up with every reason not to risk it. So, she took a deep breath and started running through the courtyard. By the time she reached the gates, which were surprisingly open, she began to question her luck.

Everything had worked in her favor. It was as though someone was making it easy for her to escape. Or that they wanted her to.

Whatever the cause, she kept running until she cleared the gates and cut off into the thick vegetation following the small river adjacent to it. She would think later about how she would find her way home. As she tore through the bushes and stepped into the water, a large figure rose out of the river, piercing her with his eyes.

Elinor halted, a silent scream erupting from her lungs. It was *him*. He stared at her as though waiting for her next move. But she couldn't move. She was rooted into the thick mud of the river bottom she was knee-deep in. He was bathing in the river, and from what she could tell, he had nothing on. His black, wet hair clung to his shoulders, water dripping down his chiseled abdomen, following a perfect line of black hair leading down into the river lapping around his waist. He raised his muscular arms up to pull the water out of his hair. And as he saw her eyes trail all over his body, a bemused expression overtook his face.

"Going somewhere?" he said, that familiar deep voice reverberating through her body. She didn't speak, weighing her options. He started walking toward her, the water rippling in his wake. "You may want to turn away." He grinned slyly as he veered to the riverbank, where she saw his clothes draped over a tree branch. Thoughts of her escape completely vanished.

Elinor did turn away, and had she not been caught off her

guard, she would have seen this as the perfect opportunity to run. But instead, she stayed rooted in the mud that had now sucked her boots into the river bottom.

He came up behind her along the riverbank, and, looking down at her with only his black breeches and boots on, he reached his hand toward her. He had now tied his hair in a knot on the top of his head. She looked at his large extended hand and, trying to shift her weight to release her boots, she realized she would need a hand if she didn't want to fall in. Defeat taking over her, she begrudgingly placed her hand in his and let him tug her to the bank. But as he did so, his grip was not met with the same force and pain as it had been the night before.

Back on dry ground, he released her hand quickly and started walking toward the castle through the bushes. She turned back to the river once more and, for whatever reason, told herself now was not the time to escape. She would bid her time and wait for another opportunity—one where he had no idea when, where, or how she managed her escape. She would also need time to map her journey home and store provisions. Her need to see her family and let them know she was okay took over all reason this morning. She could just as quickly die on her journey home as in his captivity. She needed time to prepare but hoped she did not regret leaving this opportunity behind.

Once back on the road into the castle, Elinor walked just behind her captor. She sized him up, realizing she only came up to his shoulder. His chest was at least three times as thick as hers, and he had several long scars crossing his side. *Claw marks.* His skin was also tanned, which was unusual for anyone in this land.

He looked down at her, catching her eyes on him. The same sly grin crept along his jaw. Elinor quickly turned to face the castle gates, now just steps before her. Their footsteps were the only thing breaking the silence of the morning until he finally said, "You weren't going out to catch the fresh morning air, I take it."

"No," she said firmly. They reached the courtyard by the time Elinor had formulated her plea in her head.

"Why am I here?"

"I told you. You have no right to kill the wolves here. They are for me to deal with."

"I don't understand. I helped you kill one. Why not just count it as your own and let me go?" They had reached the front door, and he stopped and turned, his hard gaze looking down at her.

"I don't expect you to understand. But you can't go home."

"But I have to!" she demanded, swallowing hard. Trying to keep her voice steady, she said, "I have a family to care for. They have nothing. Without me, there is no food. No money. I am all they have."

"They are taken care of," he said. Elinor stepped back, shock filling her.

"Wha—what do you mean, taken care of?" she said slowly, narrowing her eyes at him. Had he killed them? Had they been taken away because of her actions? He stood taller as he read the accusations clearly running across her face.

"Your family is safe, and they are provided for." Elinor turned away from him, staring back through the castle gates.

"I don't get it."

"No, I suppose you don't. And you won't. But you have to stay." He brushed his hair back off his face.

"For how long?" she asked desperately, turning back to him.

He looked intently at her and then said, "Until my work here is done."

"I could help you," Elinor blurted out, thinking it would quicken her path to freedom. His look hardened, that metallic flash shining in his eyes for the briefest moment. Then, he stepped close to her, put his fingers under her chin to tilt it to his face, and said roughly,

"Your method of killing is of no use to me."

He held her gaze a moment longer, her throat against his fingers as she swallowed. Something flashed in his eyes. Hunger, she thought. But not the hunger she had known.

Just then, the door opened before them, and his accomplices stood in the doorway, staring at them with his fingers still on her chin. They both also had long hair, although not as dark as her captor. And while they weren't as tall, they were almost equally as strong. And one of them had symbols she had never seen inked on his face. Unlike the man standing next to her, they had softer, non-threatening brown eyes.

"Christ, Darragh," one of them said with a laugh. "Let the girl breathe."

Elinor shot him a look and saw both of them smirking, but not at her. They were laughing at the brute next to her. The one without the inking on his face said,

"Couldn't manage to get your shirt on during that long walk home?" Her captor let out a growl.

"Ignore him," the other man said to Elinor, nodding to his captain. "He doesn't get out much."

The wolf hunter launched a fist right into his shoulder, but Elinor could tell it wasn't with as much force as she knew that arm could deliver.

"That's for being an envious prick," he said through gritted teeth. And then, he thrust the same force of a punch into the other man's stomach.

"And that's for letting her slip out." He nodded in Elinor's direction. Both men only winced at the impact, but all three looked as though they were going to brawl as they clenched their fists. What an absurd sight that would be, Elinor thought, with all of them huddled in that narrow entryway. But before she could get her hopes up that they would all knock each other out and she could run free, her captor flung his massive arms over both of their necks and, laughing together, they walked into the castle toward what she had thought was the dining room. The leader of the trio shot a look over his shoulder and said through a grin,

"Come and eat. You must be starved."

Elinor just gaped at the three of them, still standing in the doorway. But a small, plump woman with frizzy white hair protruding out of her cap, came from the other side of the entrance hall holding a platter of food. Seeing Elinor frozen in the doorway, she beckoned her to follow with a nod of her head.

Elinor did so, feeling the all-too-familiar hunger gnawing at her insides. She entered the room that the other men had been in earlier and found that it was indeed a large dining hall. The wooden table was long and laden with more food than Elinor had ever seen. Eggs, various meats, bread with a wide crock of butter, and fruits that certainly weren't from Galway.

The men were already pulling themselves to the table, the ornately carved wooden chairs scraping beneath their weight. The dishware was sparkling against the morning sun streaming through the small windows in the hall. The price of one of those dishes alone could feed a small family for a month, Elinor thought bitterly.

Still rooted to her spot at the end of the table, she took in the walls surrounding her. A large crest was above the fireplace, no doubt belonging to the family that had once lived here before the wolf hunters moved in. A cabinet on the opposite wall was laden with silver and porcelain dishware. But the sight that caused her jaw to drop was the ceiling. Wolf skins were suspended directly above their heads as though they were flags. There must have been thirty skins of varying grays, blacks, and whites.

She could feel her captor's eyes on her while the other two men were jesting and pulling food onto their plates. She forced her gaze onto him and, unable to stand the sight of such extravagance and greed, she turned on her heel and climbed the six stories to the room that, for now, would be hers.

...

Sometime later, with the sun now high in the sky, a small

knock broke the raging in her head. Elinor had kicked off her wet, mud-soaked boots and socks next to the door and curled up on the ornate bed, fighting the fury of her circumstance. She hated everything about it. Her inability to give her family a better life. The extravagance that only a few were allotted. The hunger that pained nearly every Irish-born person in Galway. And the fact she had no idea why she was here.

When she did not reply to the knock, the door tentatively creaked open, and the old woman peered around the corner.

"Pardon me, dear, but I thought you might like something to eat."

Elinor shifted on the bed and saw that the woman carried a small tray of food leftover from the hunter's breakfast. Her fury softened at the kind features of the woman's face. She had piercing blue eyes and supple rosy cheeks. She was short and though elderly, she seemed to move with impressive agility.

Elinor sat up in the bed and grasped the tray from the woman as she approached. Her stomach groaned in want at the sight of the food. Defiance and self-imposed starvation would not get her to her family any sooner. She took a small bite of meat and instantly wanted to ravish the entire tray. Sensing her hunger, the old lady said as she was busying herself tying back the ornate curtains,

"No need to trouble yourself with manners, dear. I know the

hunger in your eyes." And then, nodding to the plate in Elinor's lap, she added, "Eat," which she did.

Elinor ate so quickly and so heartily that she knew she would surely be sick if she did not stop. And the old lady said as much.

"Best to stop now so you don't lose it all, dear. I will leave it on the table just here for when you are ready for more." Elinor wanted to protest, but she knew the old lady was right and handed over the food. The woman then started opening up an armoire that was filled with dresses made from the loveliest fabric Elinor had ever seen. She pulled a soft blue dress out and sized it up next to her.

'The young lady who lived in this room before you was nearly your same height. I should think these will fit you nicely."

She brought it to the bed, laying it out carefully. Elinor swallowed hard.

"I cannot wear that."

"But you must, dear. You cannot stay in those clothes. They are covered in blood, sweat, and Lord only knows what else," she said, slightly wrinkling her nose. For some reason, Elinor wondered if her captor had also smelled these things on her.

"I have a bath waiting for you in the kitchen. Come," the woman said. And she opened the door and beckoned Elinor to follow. With reluctance, she did as she was told, her bare feet padding the stone steps behind the old lady.

While bathing, Elinor learned the woman's name was Mrs. Hodkins. She was employed by her captor, whom she called Captain Everard, and had traveled from England to serve him as his housekeeper. Elinor had also learned that the house had only recently been abandoned by the family who had owned it for over 300 years. They had fled in the siege.

After a thorough scrubbing until every surface of her body gleamed, Mrs. Hodkins led her back upstairs and dressed her, even brushing out her hair. When asked if she wanted it styled on her head, Elinor shook her head, seeing herself for the first time in a mirror and liking the way her honey-colored brown hair looked falling around her waist. She was never able to wear it down—her occupation of trying to survive allotted no time for vanity.

When Mrs. Hodkins left to prepare lunch, Elinor stared throughout the room. Whoever had left it had been forced to leave behind most everything, as the vanity held several hairpins, a delicate comb and brush set, and a bottle of floral-scented perfume. Elinor sprayed the scent in the room and nearly gagged at how overwhelming it was. She quickly put it back and wished she could air out the space. Settling herself in a chair by the window, she opened a few of the books that had been left on the bedside table. Her reading ability was better than most in her village but was not sophisticated enough for these books. With nothing else to occupy her time, she dove into one of the books, muddling her way through the first few paragraphs.

But her mind started to wander. Staring out the small window, she thought of the girl who once lived here, the kindness that Mrs. Hodkins had shown her, and the men downstairs. The sidekicks were fierce and brutish and yet so casual. And their leader was...well, she didn't know what he was and what to make of him. He was cruel, and yet, he wasn't.

As night fell, a soft knock came through the door, and Mrs. Hodkins peered around the corner.

"The dinner is prepared, miss, and the captain is requesting your presence."

"I will not be joining them," Elinor said firmly. Mrs. Hodkins nodded and then slid into the room to light the candles on the walls and next to her bed. Then she laid logs into the fire.

"Should you chill, light yourself a fire. The men will gladly get more wood if you burn through all of it. Just ask."

Odd, Elinor thought, but she supposed there was no one else to gather firewood since it appeared no one else was in the castle. And seeing as they liked to throw around their strength, she could see them enjoying throwing their axes into trees. As Mrs. Hodkins made her way toward the door, she said,

"If you are sure you will not come down, I will bring a tray for you."

"That is unnecessary. My stomach can't possibly take another morsel of food today." And then, as the old lady nodded and turned out of the door, she said quietly after her, "Thank you for your kindness, Mrs. Hodkins."

"Not at all, dear. Let me know if you need anything."

I need my freedom. My family. But the door closed softly behind her, and Elinor sank into the bed and fell asleep.

At some point in the early hours of the morning, hooves clattered in the courtyard and dogs barked loudly. Elinor rose out of bed and saw the three men dismounting and pulling off what looked like several skins from their horse's backs. Infuriated, Elinor threw herself back onto her bed and pulled the wool blanket over her, waiting for sleep to take over her once again.

...

The following day, Elinor stayed put in her room until sundown. She felt caged in but refused to leave the room even though she knew it was unlocked and the house was quiet. No doubt the men were sleeping after spending the entire night hunting wolves. But when she cracked the door around mid-morning, she could hear quiet chatter carrying up the stairwell. *Don't they ever sleep?*

Mrs. Hodkins had brought her breakfast and a small lunch tray, and other than relieving herself in the garderobe adjacent to her room, she did not leave the confines of the four stone walls surrounding her. Attempting to fill her time, she sat in front of the mirror, learning how to put her hair partially up in one of the beautiful combs. Pleased with her fifth attempt, she then settled back into the same book as yesterday.

But her attention was soon pulled away by approaching hooves. She darted to the small window. Two men on horseback were riding through the castle gates. Squinting her eyes to try to make out the figures as they dismounted through the clouded glass, Elinor's breath caught in her throat. She could have sworn she recognized the man. Seeing the men walk into the castle below her window, she rushed to her bedroom door and cracked it as quietly as possible to listen to the voices. Bile rose in her throat at the familiar sound of one of the harsh laughs echoing through the stairwell. *The commissioner.*

He was here, and as much as she hated him, he could get her out. Her heart began to race at the possibility that he might be her answer. What she would have to give him in return, she did not want to imagine. The men talked for some time, and by the sounds of the clanging of dishes, he would join the hunters for dinner. Elinor slunk down to the second-floor landing and sat for over an hour while the men talked. She only caught parts of the conversation, most of which had to do with grumblings in the villages about the wolf bounty being revoked from the citizens and skirmishes along the western coastline. Chairs slid back across the floor, signaling that dinner was complete. The commissioner's voice broke through the scraping.

"On a final note, you should know that two wolves were slain last week by a village girl. She is of no consequence to you, and I do not believe she will dare to do so again. In fact, she may already have fled the county, God willing. Otherwise, she will have me to answer to," he said with a quick, harsh laugh. Elinor's heart raced at the mention of her. "Aside from those two, there have been no other killings by locals."

"Where are their bodies?" her captor said darkly.

"Thrown in the barn behind my residence. I have a man who will dispose of them tomorrow. Their bodies are starting to rot," he said with a grimace in his voice.

"No," the captain said coldly. "Anluan, you will go with him to collect them. No one is to touch them."

"If you prefer," the commissioner said skeptically. Sensing the men were finished, Elinor slipped down the last set of stairs.

Heart pounding, she stepped into the dining hall to face the men. The light from the torches on the wall cast a warm glow around her. She stood taller than she felt as the wolf hides hung ominously over her. She could feel her cheeks warm with the fear of how the commissioner would react to seeing her.

But her eyes settled on her captor, who was still seated while the rest of the men stood around him. His chin was resting on his fist as he glared at her from the head of the table. But his glare wasn't menacing toward her. It was something entirely different. Suddenly, Elinor felt all too aware of what she must have looked like. She was still in the light blue dress from yesterday, her hair cascading down her back, brushing against her waist, and her petite breasts pushed up to her neck. She felt his gaze slide up and down her, even though his eyes never left hers. The commissioner's barking laugh broke the stare between them.

"I don't believe it!" he sputtered between his guffaws. "Miss Acheson, you certainly do get around." The words hung in the thick air surrounding them. Elinor saw the commissioner's assistant shift awkwardly. The two other hunters flanking either side of their leader shared bemused expressions. The commissioner walked toward her, sizing her up, hands clasped behind his back.

"You then have already learned of little Miss Acheson's impressive hunting skills, Captain. I didn't need to tell you after all. And it seems she had a way of sniffing you out as well," he said, humor in his eyes. He lifted himself up and down on his toes, as he often did when he was enjoying humiliating her. "Yes, you are cunning, girl. And I didn't know you could also pretend to be a lady. The rumors circulating through the village must be true about you."

The captain cocked his head toward her and said, "I am sure Miss Acheson holds many talents along with her hunting skills."

"Indeed, to be sure," the commissioner said jovially. "I won't presume to know why she is under your roof, but I am sure you know all too well of her...diverse talents. Or you will soon."

Elinor's face reddened even more. And then the commissioner stood right in front of her and grabbed her chin to pull it up into his hideous face.

"Tsk." He clucked his tongue. "Perhaps you will be able to get more out of her than I ever could," he said, and he ripped his hand away.

A thundering crash came from the back of the dining hall. The wolf hunter had stood so quickly that his chair was thrown back to the ground, and Elinor swore she had heard a growl erupt from his lungs.

"Apologize," he snarled.

"For what?" the commissioner said. "She always knelt willingly for me for a few coins." Then, as if wanting to deliver a final blow, he looked her slowly up and down and said, "Pity you never tried harder for me. You might have never had to get yourself in this situation in the first place." And then he left, the assistant cowering behind him. The men in the dining hall did not move until they heard hoof steps clatter out of the courtyard.

"Follow him and bring the wolves home," her captor commanded, vengeance hanging onto every word. Both men nodded, and as they passed Elinor, they offered subtle smiles—smiles that weren't laden with pity but rather just kindness. She felt lightheaded as a clang of metal sounded throughout the house. They were armoring themselves for something she did not want to imagine. As the door closed behind them, her captor studied her.

"Come eat," he said, still standing rooted to the spot where he had knocked over his chair.

Feeling lightheaded from the loss of any possible escape with the commissioner, Elinor did his bidding. Had she not felt like fainting from the disappointment, she would have been shocked by him pulling the chair out for her as she approached the table. When she didn't move to fill her plate, he took it upon himself to serve her. Her plate was heaped with food.

"I can't possibly eat all of this," she grumbled.

"You need to eat. You have been hungry for too long."

"What would you know of hunger?" she protested.

"More than you can imagine," he said darkly. Elinor just stared at her plate.

"I can't eat when I know my family is hungry."

"I told you they are provided for."

"By who?" she asked, looking him hard in the eyes. After a pause, he said,

"By me."

"Why?" she begged.

He matched the hardness of her gaze. He swirled the wine in his goblet, looking at her. The large fingers clasped around the goblet had strange inkings on them, similar to those on one of the sidekick's faces.

"Have you ever thought what Cromwell's commanders would do if they learned a woman was slaying wolves in Ireland?" His eyes narrowed on her, willing her to see his reasoning. She hadn't thought beyond providing for her family. "If word got out, you would be imprisoned by men far worse than myself. They would deem you a witch, for no woman could possibly hunt like you without using some sort of sorcery. The British government prioritizes witch hunting even more so than wolf hunting." And then, to add to his argument, he said, "You would burn at the stake. And so would your family." Cold sweat trickled down her back.

"Why do you care?" she said in almost a whisper.

He turned his eyes away, running his inked fingers thoughtfully along the carved arm of his chair.

"Because I have to," he said, his eyes distant. Elinor didn't understand and figured she likely never would.

"When will I be released?" He turned his head back to her.

"As I already said, you will be allowed to leave when our work here is done."

"So, when all wolves are killed," she said, her shoulders sinking with defeat. "That could be years."

"I am a better hunter than you give me credit for," he said, humor trickling into his voice.

"Let me help you," she said, trying again to offer her skills to quicken her road to freedom.

"No," he said firmly.

"I have proven myself more than capable of bringing down wolves. I, too, am a wolf hunter," she said, squaring her shoulders as she sat higher in her chair.

"No," he said again. When Elinor went to balk at him, he cut her off, anger rising in his voice. "As I said, my purpose in holding you here is to keep you and your family from burning at the stake. Imagine what people would say if you were now running with the most fearsome wolf hunters in Britain. I am already having a hard enough time planting seeds of gossip into that little village of yours and those surrounding it that you didn't kill those wolves."

She stared at her plate, remembering the curious looks her townsmen had given her. The rumors the commissioner had just mentioned. Her own pride in taking down those wolves had shielded her from the reality of what those looks might have really meant.

"So I am to wait idly until you have killed every wolf in Galway?" When he did not speak, she pushed her chair back with a hard scrape, drowned herself with the wine in her full goblet, and left without so much as another word.

...

Rain threatened the next morning, and Elinor could tell the past few days of sunlight would be buried in several days, if not weeks, of soggy weather. Knowing she had to do whatever she could to stay sane, she dressed and went down to the kitchens to see if she could help Mrs. Hodkins with cooking, cleaning, laundering—anything. Seeing the desperation in her eyes, Mrs. Hodkins put her to work at the fire, stirring a cauldron of stew for the coming nights. As she wiped her brow of sweat from the heat, Elinor turned to ask the woman if she had children—an attempt to make conversation. But she was caught off guard when she saw him standing in the kitchen doorway, leaning against the wall. The metal ladle in her hand clattered to the ground. Elinor cursed to herself, quickly picking it up.

He was dressed to go out riding—a black cloak tied around his neck, a slim wolf's tooth necklace dangling at his throat. She recalled that he had been wearing it when he was bathing in the river. At the time, she had just been too preoccupied with other aspects of him to pay attention to it.

He gave her a bemused expression and then said to Mrs. Hodkins, "Do you have the loaves ready?"

"Yes, captain. There, in that basket," she said, pointing toward the large basket on the table. "And I've included some fruit for the boy and several provisions from the garden out back."

"Thank you, Mrs. Hodkins. You always think of everything."

Elinor was about to blurt out her question of where he was going, but she did not want to give him the satisfaction of her curiosity. But he saw into her and raised his eyebrows, saying,

"This basket is going to your family. Would you like to send them a letter?"

She was taken aback by his offer. Of course she wanted to, but what would she say? *Imprisoned. Hope you are alive and cared for as I have been promised.* Or perhaps, *Take the money and go. I will find you one day.*

Elinor nodded in reply and set the ladle on the table in front of the fireplace. She followed him up the stairwell to the second floor into a nearly empty room. It must be where he kept his study, for there was a large desk with only one chair. He beckoned her to follow him around the desk and pulled the chair out for her to sit down. She looked quizzically at him, but he pulled out parchment and a quill from a desk drawer.

"You will need to be brief, Miss Acheson, as I have business in the town today."

Elinor nodded, and he exited the room, leaving her to stare at the blank parchment before her. She sat and thought about what she could possibly tell them that would reassure them. She settled on,

I am fine. Be home soon. - Elinor

Folding the letter and leaving the study, she walked down the stairs and out into the entrance and found him waiting there, his body blocking the doorway. He was staring out at the courtyard, and though she thought her footsteps were quiet, he must have sensed her behind him. She gave him the letter, and he tucked it into the basket.

"Not going to read it?" she asked with irritation.

He shook his head. "It is none of my business."

"I thought you were making everything about me your business."

"Only your protection. I do not think anything you say to your family will threaten that. And you took only a moment to write it, so I can't imagine you shared too many details."

"You are assuming I can write." He raised his eyebrows, a shocked expression crossing his face.

"I am sorry, I shouldn't have assumed…I just saw you reading and thought you would know."

She laughed bitterly. "Spying on me at night?" She only read in her room, so he could only know that if he had climbed up to the top level of the castle. He shifted his weight, suddenly looking different than she had ever seen him. Uncomfortable.

"You had a book lying next to the bed when I came up to check on you last night before we went hunting. I wanted to make sure that you were fine after seeing that piece of…" he trailed off, curbing his tongue.

So, he had seen her sleeping. He had cared enough about her to see that she was okay after she had left him at the table. She didn't know what to make of this. She felt an unwelcome pull in her abdomen. Silence hung between them as soft rain started to fall in the doorway behind him.

Nodding toward the letter, she said, "I just told them that I am fine and will be home soon. That's all."

He nodded. Avoiding her eyes, he pulled his hood over his head and then turned on his heel, his cloak flying out behind him as he walked toward his horse. Once mounted, he shot her a glaring stare, the metallic eyes shining through the raindrops. Elinor shivered, and it wasn't because of the rain settling on her skin as she stood in the doorway. Everything about him was unnerving.

Her captor was gone for the rest of the day, and Mrs. Hodkins had even gone out, leaving her with the two sidekicks. Avoiding her room while he was away, Elinor sat in the kitchen with a book propped against a jug, her head on her arms. Every now and then, she stood to turn the pot over the fire and then would get sucked back into her book, only a few chapters in despite the hours she had already given to it.

She was pulled suddenly from her reading when the two men came in, talking loudly about something that Elinor could not make out. They hadn't seen her and started rummaging through the small pantry, cursing the fact there was nothing to eat. Then, the younger-looking of the two spotted the stew hanging over the fire. He made to grab bowls, but Elinor cleared her throat and, startling them, said,

"Mrs. Hodkins will be very displeased if she finds out you have dipped into the evening meal she has been preparing all day."

A bowl slipped out of his hands and clattered onto the ground. His accomplice laughed at him as he quickly picked the intact bowl up and placed it back on the shelf.

"I didn't know you were here, miss. My apologies."

Elinor couldn't help but crack a smile at his surprise. He put the other bowl back and awkwardly put his hands in his pockets. It made her smile even more.

"My name is Elinor," she said. "Please call me that from now on."

A grin broke across his face. "I am Fáelán. And that is Anluan," he said, nodding his head toward the other man.

"It seems like you will be stuck with me for some time," she said, irritation dripping with every word. The two men shifted uncomfortably.

"Yes, so it seems," said Anluan.

"Nonsense," said Fáelán. "This shouldn't take us but a month —maybe less even."

"As long as Darragh doesn't purposely slow us down," Anluan said bemused, nodding in Elinor's direction.

She looked hard at him, but Anluan had a large smile across his face. The men both laughed together but not at Elinor. It was as though they were teasing their captain. It made her crack a smile again. They both sat on the bench opposite her at the table. She beckoned toward a chunk of freshly made bread and cheese sitting next to her. They both reached out eagerly for it.

"You all look so similar. And...not as I would imagine Englishmen looking," Elinor said hesitantly. "Are you all related?"

"Anulan and I are brothers," said Fáelán, quickly clearing his throat of the bread. And Darragh grew up with us, so he is basically our brother, too."

"I see," she said. "And how did you come to be wolf hunters?"

Fáelán shifted slightly on the bench, perhaps in discomfort at her question, but Anluan smiled kindly and said, "That is a story we can only properly re-tell with Darragh here." Elinor nodded again, feeling a sense of secrecy hanging between the brothers.

They sat in silence for a bit, only broken by the tearing of bread, but to Elinor's surprise, there was no awkwardness in the quiet between the three of them. Eventually, Anluan rose from the bench and left for the dining hall, returning with three ornate goblets and a pitcher of wine. Filling all three and passing them out, the two men drank heartily while Elinor sipped hers, studying them over her goblet. Fáelán let out a groan after he emptied his, and said,

"Argh, that wine is abysmal. Makes me miss home." Anluan shot Fáelán a look, and before Elinor had the chance to ask them where home was, he asked,

"I'm curious where you learned to hunt, Miss Acheson."

"Few women, and men, for that matter, can hit a target like you," Fáelán added with a smile.

Elinor took another sip from her wine, scanning them over the top of her goblet. Then, she set it down and, looking at her hands, said, "My father."

"What was he like?" Fáelán asked. And then, Elinor told them what felt like the story of her life.

She told them of how her father had taught her to hunt, how he left to fight in the war and died in a pathetic skirmish, the struggle of seeing her mother grieve and how she never really recovered, how her little brother had been robbed of the joys of childhood that she had experienced, and how she had no choice but to go out and fight every day for their survival.

Elinor had never been asked to share anything about herself, and certainly no one would have ever asked because her story was like so many others. Yet, it felt good to recount her life to someone else, even though it was likely small compared to what life these men had lived. Yet, when she finished her story with a shrug of her shoulders, the two men smiled kindly at her.

"Your father must have been a hell of a teacher because we've never seen a woman shoot like you did that night," Fáelán said seriously.

Anluan nodded in agreement and said, "Most men couldn't make that shot."

Silence sat between them again, and Elinor had the urge to ask them about their past, but before she had the chance, Fáelán clapped his hands together to dust off breadcrumbs and said,

"If there is anything you need while you are here, please just ask. We will get you anything Darragh permits." Elinor considered it and thanked them. They swung their legs over the bench and made to exit the kitchen, but then a thought came to her.

"Do either of you have a pair of breeches you aren't using?" They turned, surprise creeping across their faces.

"Why do you ask?" Anluan inquired, humored.

"I can't stand another moment in these dresses," she said, pulling the thick fabric away from her legs. Fáelán grinned broadly at her.

"I've got a pair that Mrs. Hodkins can fix up for you. I'll give them to her when she returns from the village."

Satisfied, Elinor thanked them and turned back to her book. She couldn't help but think how, for the first time in a long time, she didn't feel she had to give anything of herself in return for their willingness to help her.

...

Her captor didn't return until the evening. Elinor saw him ride through the gates from her room, and eager to learn of her family, she climbed down the stairs to ask after them. But he never came in. Instead, he waited on his horse for Fáelán and Anluan, and the three men rode off together and did not return until the following morning.

When she awoke, she saw that Mrs. Hodkins had left Fáelán's folded breeches on the end of her bed. There was also a white linen shirt, which pleased her immensely to slip into. Rinsing her face in the cool washbasin and tying her hair up in a braid, she nearly skipped down the stairs into the kitchens to thank Mrs. Hodkins.

Her gratitude was met with a warm bowl of porridge and boiled eggs. The two women chatted easily as they broke their fast at the small kitchen prep table. And then, helping clean up their dishes, Elinor told her what she planned to do that morning. She figured it would be best to be completely transparent so as not to infuriate her captor. With a gentle hand on her arm, Mrs. Hodkins warned her to stay very close to the castle walls, reminding her that it was her life that was being safeguarded. Elinor almost felt teary at the thought that someone else cared for what happened to her.

As she walked out the door, she glanced back at the empty dining hall and noted there were at least six new skins suspended from the ceiling. A lump rose in Elinor's throat. She wanted all the wolves in these lands strung up there so she could be freed, but the loss of those beautiful creatures had started ripping at her heartstrings.

Elinor grabbed the few supplies she needed and walked through the castle gates without worry of being seen. She had no desire to thwart her captor's commands, knowing that her family's safety hung in the balance. Veering off the road down a small animal slide that led to the river, Elinor pushed the vegetation out of her way. She decided to head upstream along the river, heeding Mrs. Hodkins' warning to stay close. She never lost sight of the castle walls.

Finding the perfect spot, Elinor settled down in the dirt and crafted a fishing pole for herself, sliding a small chunk of bread onto the end. Content to sit and watch the water and listen to the sounds of the forest for the rest of her day, Elinor laid back and waited for a dip in her line.

By the time the sun broke through the thick clouds over-head, she had four beautiful, glistening catches laid next to her on the bank. Her stomach started to growl at the expectation of lunch—a meal she had not had the luxury of enjoying for years. She picked a handful of berries among the bushes a little bit further upstream, leaving her lines behind.

Lost in finding more berries to bring back to the castle, she missed the birds going still. But, as the rippling of the water all of a sudden became deafening against the quiet of the forest, Elinor's blood chilled. Something was there. She stalked quietly back to where she had been fishing. How foolish she had been. Something surely had scented the fish and was lured to her spot.

Carefully peering through the last of the branches before she could see what was there, her breath caught in her throat. A small, light-grey wolf was feasting on her fish. Its head perked up in her direction as her human scent no doubt reached its nostrils. Elinor froze and stopped breathing altogether. The wolf continued to stare in her direction, but when it detected no movement, it turned back to its meal. With two fish eaten, the wolf moved to the third, but another rustle, now from the path behind it, caused the wolf to grab the other two fish in its mouth and wait. Nothing moved in the forest. If it started to run off with the fish, it would run right into her. Elinor waited for yet another wolf to emerge, preparing herself to run for her life. Time hung suspended as Elinor waited for more wolves to emerge or for this one to find her. But the silence was finally sliced by the sound of the wolf crumpling to the ground, a long knife shimmering in the sunlight amidst the thick fur coat.

With only a few strides, her captor was immediately on the wolf, but it had been killed instantly. Crouched over it with his back to her, Elinor could not see what he was doing. But then he roared out into the forest.

"Anluan!" In a matter of moments, Anluan and Fáelán both came running to the site of the fallen wolf. They already knew what to do.

"Do it quickly," her captor said darkly. Anluan picked up the wolf in his arms and stalked back downstream toward the road, Fáelán trailing him.

Her captor watched them go and then said quietly, "Come out, Miss Acheson."

Elinor swallowed and then pushed the branches from her body and walked up next to him. His face was seething, his eyes metallic, and his chest rising and falling. He looked disheveled, no doubt from being up all night. Standing over her, he looked down at her.

"You were foolish."

"I know," she said quietly. She had been. She knew better than to leave fresh kill out. "I didn't think they would be out during the day. Or so close to the castle."

"No, you didn't think," he said coldly.

She hated him for making her feel so small. Finding her voice, she said, "I just wanted to be outside. To be useful."

And she had. She was attempting to catch the fish for their dinner—to give Mrs. Hodkins a break. She couldn't take his furious looks anymore and gathered the few supplies she had, tossed the remaining bread into the creek, and started walking back to the road. She could feel his eyes still on the back of her.

He stalked her all the way back to the courtyard, where she set her supplies down and began to make her way into the house.

"Wait," he commanded.

She turned to look at him. He sized her up and down, a glimmer of something in his eyes. Perhaps it was humor for how she was dressed in Fáelán's old pants. Perhaps it was pity for her stupidity.

"Come with me," he said, turning toward the stables. Reluctantly, she followed him and watched as he readied his horse. Then he disappeared into the house for a moment. Re-emerging, he had a bow and quiver of arrows in one of his hands. Her breath caught in her throat. It was *her* bow—the one they had taken from her when he had first captured her. He set the weapons on the ground and then, without asking, lifted her right off of her feet and onto his horse's back. Then, he handed her the bow and quiver and threw himself over the horse, settling in behind her. His own bow was strapped to his back, along with a knife sheathed on his leg.

He snapped the reins on his horse, and they rode through the gates of the castle, veering off into the forest. They rode hard along the opposite bank of the river for several minutes until the trees became so dense he slowed the horse to a walk. Elinor's senses were ablaze. Pinned against him as they swayed back and forth on the horse's back, Elinor could feel her backside pushing into his hips, the firm chest muscles cradling her head. One of his arms was gripped around her middle. Her mind wandered to the first morning where she stumbled across him bathing in the river.

Finally halting with a low "whoa," he dismounted and tied the horse off to a tree. Then he lifted Elinor down before she could shift her weight to slip down alone.

"We go on foot now," he said. Elinor looked perplexed. Seeing her confusion, he cocked his head to one side and said, "I thought you might like to go hunting."

A smile crept across her face—the first she had ever given him, and she nodded toward his outstretched hand that told her to lead the way into the forest. They walked slowly, listening intently to every sound. When anything stirred, she froze, and he would close in behind her, sometimes grabbing an arrow out of her quiver and handing it to her. They wound their way deeper into the forest, crossing several small streams, sometimes catching glimpses of the sea adjacent to them in the distance.

In all, Elinor killed nearly a dozen small game. Her captor had tied them all on a long string, hauling them for her and letting her take the lead. Never once did he pull out his own bow that was strapped to his back. He just watched her, sometimes slowing her and pointing to something she may have missed. She had rarely used a bow to hunt small game, but it gave her an incredible thrill—one that she never experienced with trapping. As the sunlight began to fall in long bands between the branches of the trees, he finally broke the silence.

"We should go back."

She turned to face him and saw his eyes roam all over her. It was as though he was seeing her for the first time. She looked down at herself. Her bow clasped in her hand. Her thick braid grazing her waistband. The quiver strap nestled between her breasts. Her face glistening with sweat. The satisfaction of a good hunt spreading through her body.

"Yes, I think I have had enough killing for today," she said. He looked as though he wanted to say something, but when nothing came out of his mouth, Elinor walked around him and started following their path back to his horse.

The ride home was quiet again, but the route was different. When Elinor noticed the shift in their journey, she broke the silence, saying,

"I thought we were headed back to the castle."

"A slight detour—it will only be a moment."

And when they emerged onto a road from the forest, she saw a small gathering of cottages with children playing amongst the houses. He slowed the horse and hopped down, leading it to a communal space around a fire in front of the cottages. The children hid behind stone walls as he approached, but an older woman with a babe on her hip walked toward him, a smile spread across her cracked face.

Elinor couldn't hear the words that passed between them and only realized the purpose of their mission when he was walking back. He had left every animal she had killed for the people in that tiny village. By the time he had slipped in behind her, several more women came out of their houses, waving their thanks, and the children ran after them as they made their way back onto the road.

Elinor wracked her brain for answers. *Who was he?* She didn't understand him at all. He was fierce and had an air of cruelty, especially when those eyes shifted. But there was something else—something that, whether she wanted to admit it or not—was drawing her in. As that realization hit her, she felt her body sinking more into his and his arm instantly gripped tighter around her. The horse also slowed without a word from its master, as though it sensed this ride should last longer.

The sun had long set when Aughnanure finally rose up on the horizon. When he lifted her off the horse, he slid her down his body slowly.

"You did well today, Miss Acheson," he said sincerely, looking down at her. "You did a wonderful thing for those families."

"Thank you for the hunt," she said back. Taking off her quiver and handing her bow to him, he shook his head and reached for her hand that was gripping the weapon.

"It's yours, Miss Acheson. Keep it with you."

Elinor looked down at her father's bow, realizing the freedom he was giving her in having this. She nodded and then said, "My name is Elinor. Please call me that."

He nodded. "Only if you call me Darragh."

"Darragh," she said softly, trying the name out on her lips. She had tried his name out in his head when she first heard it but had never dared to say it. She could tell he was about to say something, but then Anluan and Fáelán came out of the castle walls, dressed in their hunting leathers, weapons in hand.

"Nice to finally see you two," Fáelán said, looking between the two of them with a glint of humor in his eyes. Darragh shifted his weight and stood up straighter with a glare in his eyes. Fáelán's humor in the whole thing didn't falter.

"We should go, Darragh," Anluan said seriously. Darragh nodded and caught the extra knife that Anluan tossed in his direction. "Mrs. Hodkins has dinner set for the two of you in the dining room, Elinor."

Darragh cocked his head in Anluan's direction, assessing the familiarity between them. Anluan just shrugged his shoulders under the glare and strode to the stables. These two clearly were unaffected by the power Darragh seemed to wield over everyone else.

Elinor turned, leaving the men to ready themselves for their hunt. But as she walked into the castle, she could feel Darragh's eyes on her until she closed the door behind her.

As Elinor tried to sleep that night, her muscles ached with pain from their hunt that day. Much to her frustration, her body had softened in the short time she had been confined. Memories flashed in her mind of the stalking, riding, and killing—and of Darragh, behind her through it all. As she tried to fall asleep, she did whatever she could to push another aching in her body—one that was wholly foreign and yet all too natural.

When she finally gave in to sleep, her slumber was only broken by the soft creak of her door as the sky was beginning to lighten through her window. She knew it was him. She could *feel* him. But she didn't stir.

...

As the late summer gave way to autumn and the nights grew longer, Elinor sensed a shift in the men. Over seventy wolf skins hung above their heads as they all dined together at the long table, even Mrs. Hodkins. Their hunting trips, often lasting several days, yielded only one or two skins upon their return. Elinor sensed their time in Galway was drawing to a close, as they had to venture farther for fewer wolves. Her liberation was within reach.

Yet, she couldn't ignore the truth that the weeks at Aughnanure Castle had been some of the best of her life since her father had died. She tried to ignore the guilt that rose in her chest at this realization.

Every day, she started her mornings with Mrs. Hodkins, preparing the day's meals and often making bread baskets to take to the small community where she and Darragh had stopped after their first hunt together. Since then, they had hunted together nearly every day after he had returned, and when he was away, she joined Mrs. Hodkins in her trips to the village near Aughnanure. Darragh had deemed it safe for her to start going out and to look like she was employed by him to help dispel any further myths about her being a witch. On her first few trips, few people made eye contact with her. But now, she had friendly relationships with most.

Darragh, Anluan, and Fáelán now took turns delivering food baskets to her mother and brother. They had told her that Conor was setting his own traps now and even made his first sale after catching an extra hare one night. Elinor couldn't have been prouder and yet, she felt guilty that she hadn't been there to see him do it the first time. But she knew it was best not to go home until there were no more whispers in her own village. Some people were reluctant to give up on the idea of her being a witch, as she had long been a little too different for most.

It was after Fáelán had told her about Conor's first sale that Elinor wandered down to the river to contemplate the coming changes. Not only were the men starting to make plans to leave for England again when they didn't think she was listening, but she was facing the reality that she had been living a protected life of luxury—despite being held against her will. For the first time in years, Elinor did not have to fight for survival every single day. She didn't have to carry the responsibility of keeping her mother and brother alive. And she didn't have to make the call that they stay in Galway, their home, or leave for a freer life.

Perched on the ground where she had fished that day several weeks ago, she found her thoughts were broken by the soft crushing of leaves beneath boots. Elinor turned and saw Darragh twisting between branches to reach her. He sat on the ground next to her, picked up a stick, and began shredding it into small pieces. Elinor turned back to the river as they sat in silence. They had grown used to being this way with one another—being together in the silence of the woods. She waited for him to break the silence, but he never said anything, and she didn't either. So many words were trying to pour out of her, and yet, she welcomed the silence and savored the comfort of being near him—this man whom she once detested for taking away her freedom and now resented for showing her a better life. And maybe even something more.

...

When the incessant rains of autumn slid over Galway, Elinor knew the day had come. The men had not hunted that night, and when she walked into the dining hall the following morning, she found all three of them with their heads bowed over a map. Fáelán and Anluan shot her smiles when she walked toward the table, and the former pulled out a chair for her. Darragh just looked at her, a glimmer of something unnerving in his eyes. He must be in a mood, she thought. Elinor had started learning the different shifts in his eyes depending on his temper. She had never seen anything like it. She knew the others saw the changes in his eyes, too, but they never flinched or balked at this strangeness. Fáelán clapped her on the shoulder and said,

"Well, little huntress, it looks like our work here is finished."

Elinor surveyed the three of them as he said this. Anluan

leaned back in his chair with his large arms crossed over his chest and said with a smile,

"Conor can't wait for you to get home." She smiled back at him, trying to focus on the joy of seeing her little brother and mother.

"We haven't seen hide nor hair of a wolf in the past week. It seems they have all been freed," Anluan said.

Elinor thought this was an odd way of describing killing off an entire species in a territory. But Anluan was a bit of a mystery, being the more pensive and cerebral of the two brothers. Fáelán tossed him a look of judgment, but Anluan just shrugged. Darragh kept his eyes on the now rolled-up map.

"When do you leave?" she said, trying to keep her voice steady.

The two brothers looked to Darragh to respond. Keeping his eyes on the table, he said,

"One week." Elinor nodded, trying to catch his gaze, but he did not look up. "Mrs. Hodkins has quelled any rumors around you being a witch, so you are also free. As promised," Darragh said quietly.

She should have pushed herself away from the table on Darragh's words and rushed up the stairs to pack what few belongings she had. That would be the response of a captive yearning to get home. But she just nodded and started forcing herself to eat from the plate in front of her.

Anluan began discussing a plan for a dinner they would host at the end of the week to signal their departure. He was running through a list of names of various British officials in the area to commemorate the end of wolves in Galway. Fáelán chimed in about making it a dance with some hired musicians he had seen in the city. Anluan remarked that few British women had come with their husbands, making the idea of a dance out of the question. But Fáelán insisted that he could find plenty of women and wine to make the night merry. Anluan grumbled about it being a waste of time, and Darragh still kept his eyes on the map, his inked fingers clutching the arms of his chair.

Unable to be in their company any longer, Elinor excused herself and, grabbing her cloak, headed out of the castle doors. She had to walk, to think, to process what was running through her mind. She had never felt a part of anything. But here, something felt right. As though she somehow belonged here. She felt bonded in some way to them these past three months, and now it was like leaving...*friends*. Well, she wasn't sure she could call Darragh a friend. She didn't know what to think about him, but certainly the other two. And Mrs. Hodkins, of course. But when she thought about Darragh leaving, a pit groaned in her chest, trailing up to her throat and her eyes. There were no words to describe what he had become to her.

Winding her way downstream along the river, Elinor sat on

a log beside the water. The mist began to seep through her cloak. But it didn't matter to her in this moment. The cool wetness made her feel alive when part of her felt like it was dying off. She had half a mind to curl up and stay there until nightfall to avoid the pain of saying goodbye.

But no sooner was she soaked to the bone when Anluan eventually wandered onto the path to where she was and leaned onto the log next to her. She didn't meet his eyes, and he didn't speak. It was like that with him, much like it was with Darragh. But with Darragh, words and feelings were always coursing through her, and she had a sense that it was the same for him. Anluan was just there with her, his steadiness grounding her.

Anluan did break the silence eventually, though, and to her surprise, said,

"If you have something you need to say, you should say it. Living with unsaid words in your heart isn't living." Elinor nodded, clenching her jaw to avoid it from quivering.

"You know from experience?" she asked. Anluan nodded subtly but didn't say more.

"What if I don't know what my heart is saying?"

"Listen to it. Give it time to speak."

"And if I don't have time?"

"It will speak at the right time."

Elinor wanted to trust that he was right, but she felt something was screaming inside her already, and even though she was trying to listen, it never made any sense to her. That's why she had come to the river so often in the past few weeks—to try to let it make sense to her—but it just kept twisting in her mind.

Eventually, Anluan stood and held out his hand for her, helping her stiff body off the log. As Elinor moved, she realized how cold she had become. Together, they walked back to the castle, barely visible now amidst the rain pelting down on them.

"We're going to all miss you, little huntress," Anluan said as they finally made it into the courtyard. Elinor looked at him, surprised by the sentiment. Anluan was not one for emotions. Unable to reply without showing her heart, she nodded and forced a smile.

Climbing the stairs on her numb feet, she reached the top landing and walked into her room. A fire was already roaring. Without taking off her wet clothes, she sank in front of the fire and let her tears fall softly. She wanted to cry out, but the cold had seized her voice. Shivering wracked her body, but she didn't care. The heartache masked any physical discomfort. She eventually wore out and gave into the blackness.

Sometime later, when the veil of night had settled through

her window, the door slowly opened. Elinor heard the soft creak in the distance and shifted her head that had been turned to the fire to see who had entered. Mrs. Hodkins had come with dinner.

"Oh my dear!" she exclaimed, setting the platter of food roughly on the table next to her. "What is wrong with you? You will be sick if you do not get out of these clothes!"

She scrambled to help Elinor get out of her cloak and boots. When she had peeled off the breeches and linen shirt, leaving her naked in front of the fire, Mrs. Hodkins grabbed the thick woolen blanket on her bed and pulled a chair in front of the fire.

She heard Mrs. Hodkins mutter something about a seemingly clever and capable girl being so foolish as she laid out all of Elinor's clothes to dry. Then she grabbed a brush and started detangling her rain-soaked hair so that it fell straight down the blanket around her shoulders. Still fussing around the room, she pulled the linens back on her bed and told her before she slipped out the door that she was to eat and put herself to bed. Elinor nodded slowly, keeping her eyes on the fire. But she didn't touch her food.

At least an hour later, Mrs. Hodkins bustled back in, stoking the fire and adding another log. She just clicked her tongue when she saw Elinor was still wrapped in the blanket, the food left untouched and cold next to her.

"I am off to bed. You best eat and get yourself in that bed." Her tone softened as she said this, and she gently laid her hand on Elinor's shoulder. Without another word, she left, closing the door quietly behind her.

Elinor had never been like this. And, as she tired of staring at the sputtering flames assailing the newest log, she felt anger rise up in her chest. Her life had been hard before she had come to Aughnanure castle, to these people, but it had been hers. And everything about this place was not hers. The anger was purely at herself, for giving up her fight, for giving up on her own dreams and letting new ones—impossible ones—creep in.

Unable to sit a moment longer now that she had come to her senses, her mind became shockingly still. She never allowed herself to cry, but she remembered her mother telling her when her father had died that sometimes all one needed was a good cry." And now that she'd had that cry, she could move on.

Elinor rose from the chair with the blanket wrapped tightly around her still-naked body. Her feet were cold on the stones beneath her as she padded to the window and looked out at the cloak of night. She knew one day she would welcome the freedom of hunting again at nightfall with no one to answer to. But then she thought of the night she was captured and how she would never fear anything in the forest as much as she feared being captured by him that night. Elinor could still picture his strong body crouched over the slayed wolf and then those metallic eyes settling on her. She shivered again.

And then, as though her thoughts conjured him, the door to her room creaked open, and he stood in the doorway. That same figure that she had once feared and hated, but now could not fathom living without.

Darragh's eyes glowed in the firelight as they settled on her standing next to the window. Any decent man would turn away, seeing she was unclothed save for a blanket. But there was nothing customary about him. And as they stared one another down across the room, Elinor felt an invisible string tugging her to him.

As though her body was no longer her own and something else was controlling her movements, she found herself flowing toward him. Darragh slowly closed the door behind him and met her in front of the fire. Staring down at her, his eyes shifted to their brightest blue, the dark, wavy, long hair casting them in shadows. He lifted his fingertips to her hair and brushed it off her face. Then, he trailed his fingers down her arm, still covered by the blanket. A deep breath swelled her chest.

He grazed his other hand on her shoulder, his eyes still holding her gaze in the firelight dancing between them.

"Do you want me to leave?" he whispered.

Elinor shook her head slowly, her eyes heavy once again with emotion that she wouldn't let fall. Darragh tucked her head into his chest and stroked her back, brushing her hair with his finger-tips as it cascaded to her buttocks. She listened to his steady heart pounding in her ear. Slowly, she lifted her hand through the blanket and placed it on his chest. Then, she touched the wolf tooth hanging from his neck. He looked down at her, his gaze intense. Still holding the tooth necklace, she pulled his neck with it to bring his face closer to hers. He brushed the softest kiss against her lips. Then he did it again. And when she drew the wolf tooth closer to her, he kissed her harder. She let go of the necklace and reached around his neck, his hair tumbling around them as they remained rooted to one another.

Darragh's fingertips began pulling the blanket away from her shoulder ever so slightly. The whisper of his fingers on her bare skin sent a spark through her body—a spark that settled some-where deep within her. With each brush, the spark grew, and her kisses matched the intensity of the fire being stoked inside her. But he didn't rush and didn't match that urgency she felt grow-ing within her. His breath remained steady. At one point, he closed his eyes as though trying to suppress something within him. Elinor tried to read him, but her experience with men outside of servicing them was nonexistent. She knew nothing beyond what the old woman in the marketplace had taught her.

And, thinking that was what she should do next, she pulled back from his face. She didn't mind doing this for him. Indeed, she couldn't help but want to do it for him—something she had vowed to never have to do again.

Slowly reaching a hand out from her blanket while using the other to keep herself covered, she began to pull at the strings on his breeches. She could feel the hardness pulsing beneath the black cloth. He gave a sharp intake of air, which Elinor took as a sign that she was doing the right thing. As she pulled the laces free, she began to drop to her knees. Because of his height, she would have to put something underneath her to be able to reach him.

But when she looked up at his face, his features had shifted. All of a sudden, fury washed over his face, and his eyes turned to a roiling silver that she had never seen—well, she had only seen it once when the commissioner had taunted her in front of them. Elinor drew back, studying his face from the floor. His muscles tensed. It was as though he had become an animal. He growled at her as he plucked her off the ground like she was a small child.

"You will never do that again!" he seethed through gritted teeth.

His breath heaved in his thick chest, and his veins protruded in his neck, one throbbing in his forehead. His fists were clenching and unclenching after he let go of her.

"I am sorry," Elinor stammered, still staring at his roiling eyes. "I thought that's what you would want," she said quietly. His body froze, his fists now clamped shut.

"You thought that's what I *wanted*?" he growled. She nodded, stepping back from him now. "You have no idea what I want," he said again through gritted teeth. Elinor swallowed, her breath ragged in her chest.

"You could tell me what you want," she said carefully, knowing that it might be the thing that would send him thundering down the stairs. But something in him softened, just slightly, and she could see him reaching for something—anything—to help him contain himself. Searching his eyes for an answer, she could see the metal slowly shifting to a cool blue.

"What I want is for you to never have to do that to a man again." He took a deep breath. "What I want is to never see you feel like you have to do *anything* for a man." He started walking toward her, looking down at her again. "What I want is for you to know how strong, and fierce you are. To know how beautiful you are." He brushed her cheek with his fingertips. "I want you to know that you deserve to be the most important person in the world to someone, to know that you are their everything." Elinor's breath was trapped in her throat. She leaned into his hand on her cheek. Holding her face with both hands now, he said, "I want you to never bow to anyone again."

And as he said it, he kissed her on her forehead, down her neck, down her bare shoulder. She felt her grip on the blanket loosen with each caress of his lips. Eventually, she let it slide off her body, falling in a puddle around her feet. He wrapped her naked body in his muscled arms, burying his face in her hair. Circling her arms around his neck, Darragh quickly ran his hands down her sides and grabbed her buttocks, squeezing them softly at first and then firmly. Lifting her effortlessly off her feet, he wrapped her legs around his abdomen, and his mouth found hers. Their kisses, which were once soft and gentle, were now hungry and aching with need. Their tongues found one another, creating a dance in and out of their mouths, his hands squeezing her buttocks and pulling her harder into his embrace.

Slowly, he carried her to the bed. Laying her down gently on her back, he sunk to his knees. Elinor's heart raced in her chest as she sat up to find his face level with her thighs. She wanted to clamp her legs shut, but he forced her to remain open, his eyes staying on hers the whole time.

"What I want," he whispered, "is to kneel for you."

And he tore his eyes slowly from hers and trailed them down her body. First, they settled on her breasts, their soft rise aching for his hands, his mouth. But he just shook his head slowly, as though saying he would get to them soon. His gaze then traveled down her tight abdomen to settle between her legs. His now bright blue eyes softened and dilated at the sight of her.

"You are beautiful," he whispered.

Slowly pushing Elinor back onto the bed with his inked fingers that had reached out to her breast, Darragh began to kiss her on the most intimate part of her body. His kisses were brief as he began to slide his tongue on either side of the silken flesh between her thighs—his tongue swirling from time to time on that flesh at her center. Elinor's legs weakened at his caresses, and recognizing it, he placed her legs over his shoulders. She instantly tightened them to close around him.

"I promise you want to keep your legs open," he said wickedly. Elinor relaxed at the sight of the delight that spread across his face.

As his movements became predictable, Elinor felt that fire of desire spread throughout her pelvis, causing her to sink into the bed fully and let it take over her body. She began to pant with each swirl of his tongue. He then began to draw her into his mouth more, creating a rhythmic pressure that made her so delirious with pleasure that she thought she might take flight out of her body. And, as his movements intensified and the pleasure built within her body, Elinor felt like he was feasting on her— like a wolf devouring its kill. She tried to draw herself away from him, not knowing what was happening to her body. But he just said between his caresses,

"Stay with me."

And when he tugged on her with his teeth ever so gently, Elinor left her body entirely. She felt as though she were hovering over the bed in this flight of pleasure that burst from his mouth and out in all directions. Her arched back told him that she had reached her climax, but he kept her firmly in his mouth until she collapsed back into herself, her body limp with deliverance.

When Elinor finally opened her eyes and saw Darragh hovering over her, she gave him a smile that conveyed the deliciousness she had just experienced. He matched her smile, a hint of wickedness in it. And as he wiped his mouth with the back of his hand, she reached to pull his waist into her. But he shook his head, his hair swaying back and forth as it fell between them. He then kissed her softly and growled seductively,

"I'm not done with you."

Kicking off his boots and crawling over the bed to seat himself against the pillows, he beckoned her to him. Elinor slid up to him and, intending to sit on him, she started to place her legs on either side of him. But he shook his head and twisted her around, pressing her back against his chest. She rolled her head across him, savoring the wet kisses he placed on her temple. His fingertips began to brush against her breasts, circling each soft mound, his thumbs taunting each nipple. Elinor squirmed underneath his touch, unsure how to interpret the pleasure. Darragh grinned against her hair, knowing what his taunting was doing to her. And then he trailed both hands down her abdomen and thighs, drawing her legs up and spreading them toward the glow of the fire.

Darragh clasped her breast, holding it firmly in his hand while the other walked his fingers up her thigh to settle between her legs. As his fingertips met that silken flesh, she gasped. His touch sent more sparks through her.

"Your body is now going to be more responsive. This time, it will happen more quickly," he whispered in her ear. And not knowing what else to do, she nodded as his fingers started caressing her, sliding against her wetness.

He was right. His touch instantly sent heat through her body. He held her tightly against his chest as his caresses became quicker and more rhythmic, and, in a matter of moments, she took flight from her body again, drifting somewhere above them, above the castle—somewhere in the night sky. His continued movements kept her afloat there, and her pelvis lifted toward the ceiling. When she eventually came back down, his fingers slowed until they stilled, cupping her as she came back to her own body. And to his.

Elinor was limp from the pleasure, unable to move beyond the rising and falling of her chest. She breathed in the scent of the forest on him, the pine and woodsmoke. She felt his aching hardness pushing into her back. And as she moved against it, he let a groan escape his throat. Somehow, the throbbing between her legs was demanding more, and as she shifted to look at him beneath her eyelashes, desire flashed in his eyes. She twisted onto her side and ran the back of her fingers along the length of him beneath his breeches. He took in a sharp breath, his eyes rolling back. She did it again, and he bit his lip. Bringing his eyes back to her, he stiffened and reached for her wrist, pulling it away from him.

"You don't want me," Elinor said, trying to keep the disappointment from her voice.

Darragh shook his head slightly and said through gritted teeth, "I want you more than anything in this life. But you are not mine to take." And then, his resolve washing over him, he sat up and held her face between his hands. "Elinor, you are no one's to take. Until you choose who is worthy of you."

"What if I choose you?" she whispered. She saw sadness wash over him as he shook his head.

"I do not deserve you."

"I can judge that for myself," she said.

Darragh pulled her into his chest. "You know nothing of me and the life I live." And dropping his voice to a whisper, he said, "You deserve much more than the life I can offer you."

Elinor wanted to challenge him, to make him give her a real reason for why he wasn't enough for her, but all the fight in her to argue was gone after what he had done to her. Perhaps he had intended it to be that way. As she slid into sleep against his chest, both of them wrapped in the covers of her bed, she dreamt that he whispered *I am yours* into her hair.

...

They held each other all night, Elinor sleeping like she never had in her whole life. And when she woke, she saw he had not moved once, his eyes still looking at her as they did when she had finally given into sleep. She knew he had not slept. But at the sight of her eyes, bright with rest, he smiled playfully and moved his fingers down to pleasure her again. But the reality of what was coming that day made her slowly pull his hand back up to her chest, and she wrapped herself tighter in his arms.

When the sounds of Mrs. Hodkins bustling around downstairs reached her bedroom, Darragh unwrapped his arms from her and sat up, running his hands through his hair. He smiled softly at her and said,

"It's time to go home."

Elinor nodded, an aching rising up in her throat. But she swallowed it down and, pulling the blanket around her, she rose from the bed. Reaching for her clothes, she was glad to know they had somehow dried out in front of the fire overnight.

Darragh rose off the bed as well and strode to the armoire. He opened the door and pulled the dresses out, laying them on the bed. He smiled again at her, saying,

"These are yours now. And anything in this room. It's all yours to take home." Elinor nodded, wanting nothing of it. Staring around her, she took inventory of the things in the room. Books. Delicate hair clips. Satin heeled shoes. None of it belonged in the life she was returning to. She wandered over to the bed, fingering a soft pink dress.

"You would be breathtaking in that, but I prefer you in breeches," he grinned. Elinor smirked at him, but he came up to her and, grasping her chin to pull her face to his, he said, "Seriously. I prefer you to look exactly the way you did when I first saw you in the forest, stalking your first wolf."

"You saw me that night?" she said, searching him. He nodded. The eyes on her that first night that she had sworn were watching her in between the trees. They were his that she felt.

...

Elinor was numb as they rode out of the gates of Aughnanure castle. Pressed against Darragh's chest for one last ride with Fáelán and Anluan flaking their sides, Elinor tried to live for each breath and not dread the last they would take together.

Saying goodbye to Mrs. Hodkins had nearly done her in, but Elinor let a wall build up in her, keeping her emotions in—a wall she realized had always been up in her until Darragh had brought it crashing down within her. And if she was truthful, Anluan and Fáelán's friendship also had torn it down, stone by stone. If she focused too much on it, she felt as though she would shatter.

When the forest started to look familiar to her, Anluan and

Fáelán rode ahead of them, Darragh pulling his horse to a slower pace. The two brothers had her new possessions strapped to the backs of their horses. She figured they would be dropping them off before she arrived.

Elinor resolved to focus on the joy of being reunited with her brother and mother. She knew Conor would be different—older and prouder, even if only a few months had passed. And her mother, she imagined she would be relieved to see her, but she wasn't sure how she would fully respond to her being home again, making the decisions and supporting them.

As they eventually neared the edge of the forest near her home, Darragh slowed his horse to a halt. He hopped off his horse and lifted her to the ground. Looking down at her, he reached for her bow and quiver that had been secured to the horse and put it over her shoulder. Then he grabbed her hand and walked with her, pulling the horse along with them to the very edge of the forest. Her family's little cottage came into view in the small valley below them, along with her neighbor's homes. Smoke was coming out of most of the chimneys. Mist hung near their heads. An afternoon rain was surely coming.

She gripped Darragh's hand tightly, turning toward him. He looked down at her and, releasing the horse, he reached into his pocket. He pulled out a small package wrapped in wool and tied with string.

"For you," he said through a deep, broken voice. Elinor looked up at him, swallowing her emotions. She unwrapped the tiny package. Out fell a wolf's tooth, strung with black thread. Her breath caught in her chest. She thumbed it over in the palm of her hand. It was just like his.

"Taken from your first wolf. To remind you of how fierce you are." He picked it up from her hand and slipped it over her head, lifting her hair out of the way. The tooth felt hot as it rested against her chest. She knew she would never take it off. He pulled her close to him, his hand on the back of her neck, the other curling around her waist.

Elinor wanted to beg him to stay, to take her, to choose her. But if she opened her mouth and spoke the words of her heart, she knew she would crack into a hundred pieces at his feet when he told her no. Darragh pulled her into him, hugging her tightly, and then kissed her forehead. Breathing in his scent one last time, she pulled out of his arms and began her descent down the hill. That invisible string tugged her back to him with every step.

She could already see that Conor had come out of the house, no doubt alerted of her homecoming from Fáelán and Anluan when they rode ahead. He started running to her, and, seeing the joy on his face, she started running toward him as well. And once they were in one another's embrace, once she had assessed how he had grown over her summer away, once she had seen her mother's smiling face emerge from the small cottage door, she turned back to the hill. Darragh, Anluan, and Fáelán were standing there in a line, arms crossed over their chests, watching the reunion.

Elinor turned to meet her mother's warm embrace, and when she glanced back at the hilltop, they were gone.

About the Author

Mrs. Walker is a wife, mother of three, nurse, and historical romance writer. Her journey into the realm of historical romance was a natural extension of her deep-rooted fascination with the past. With a profound love for British history, she finds herself effortlessly transported to a world of courtly intrigues, sweeping landscapes, and timeless love stories. Her writing not only demonstrates meticulous research of the past but also weaves narratives that will sweep you across the centuries and leave you aching for a bygone era.

When her mind wanders, it invariably lands somewhere between the 15th and 19th centuries, crafting romantic storylines featuring intelligent and slightly headstrong heroines and men who bear an uncanny resemblance to her own husband.